Thomas G. Taaffe

A History of St. John's College

Fordham, N.Y

Thomas G. Taaffe

A History of St. John's College
Fordham, N.Y

ISBN/EAN: 9783337399757

Printed in Europe, USA, Canada, Australia, Japan

Cover: Foto ©Andreas Hilbeck / pixelio.de

More available books at **www.hansebooks.com**

A History

of

St. John's College, Fordham, N. Y.

By

Thomas Gaffney Taaffe, A.B.

New York

The Catholic Publication Society Co.

12 East 17th Street

London: Burns & Oates, Limited

1891

To

THE REVEREND JOHN SCULLY, S.J.

PRESIDENT OF ST. JOHN'S COLLEGE, FORDHAM, N. Y.

THIS VOLUME IS RESPECTFULLY DEDICATED.

PREFACE.

To my mind an introduction to a book of this nature seems hardly necessary. It should introduce itself. I will say, however, that in preparing this work I have endeavored to place before my readers, in an entertaining manner, such matter connected with St. John's as appeared to me to be of historic value or interest. If I have succeeded in holding their attention through a perusal of my book, I shall feel that my labor has not been in vain.

I take this opportunity of expressing my gratitude to those who have assisted me in the prosecution of this work. My thanks are due in an especial manner to the Reverend John Scully, S.J., president of St. John's College, Fordham, and the Reverend Joseph Zwinge, S.J., also of St. John's; to the Reverend P. F. Dealy, S.J.; Mr. J. J. Costello, of Cayuga, N. Y.; General Martin T. McMahon, General James R. O'Beirne, Mr. Joseph Kinney, Mr. Charles M. Walcott, of the Lyceum Theatre Company, New York; Professor J. F. Edwards, of Notre Dame University, Notre Dame, Ind.; Mr. Edward C. O'Brien, Secretary of the Alumni Association, and Dr. James N. Butler.

THE AUTHOR.

CONTENTS.

A HISTORY

OF

ST. JOHN'S COLLEGE,

FORDHAM.

CHAPTER I.

FORDHAM COLLEGE OF TO-DAY.

THE first half-century of the brilliant and successful career of Fordham College is now complete. The 24th day of June, 1891, finds that institution fifty years old, and the occasion has been befittingly commemorated by the erection on the college lawn of a handsome bronze statue of the illustrious founder of the college, the late Archbishop John Hughes, of New York. The statue is the gift of the Alumni Association, and other friends of the college. It is the work of the well-known sculptor, William Rudolf O'Donovan, and is in every respect worthy of that conscientious artist. It represents the Archbishop, clad in his episcopal robes, book in hand, in the act of delivering an address. The pose is easy, natural, and dignified, and the long cloak, falling in graceful folds from the shoulders, effectively sets off the commanding figure.

The statue is eight feet two inches high, and is mounted on a granite pedestal, bearing the following inscription:

IOANNI · HVGHES

NEO · EBORACENSIVM · ARCHIEPISCOPO

FORDHAMENSIS · LYCEI · AVCTORI

ALVMNORVM · COETVS · AMICI · BENEMERENTES

AERE · COLLATO

EXIMIO · BONARVM · ARTIVM · FAVTORI

PRAECLARE · DE · RELIGIONE · MERITO

POSVERVNT

VIII · KAL · IVL · MDCXXXXI

ANNO · L · A · LYCEO · CONDITO

The total height of the monument is eighteen feet nine inches.

Fordham College of to-day is indeed a beautiful place, but to one who, in addition to its natural beauties, finds every foot of ground, every rock and tree, every nook and corner of its time-stained walls reminiscent of some little incident of the happy days of long ago, it becomes a veritable Arcadia. What old student, returning, can gaze on the familiar scenes without a pang of regret for the days that are no more, and the pleasures and companions that, alike, are but memories of a dim, uncertain past.

But apart from the charm it possesses in the eyes of its loving children, Fordham stands pre-eminent among institutions of its kind for the picturesqueness of its surroundings, unrivalled in the beauty of its grounds. Less than a dozen miles from the heart of the great metropolis, it might be leagues away from the " busy hum of men," such is the peace and quietude that pervade the spot.

A half-hour's ride from the Grand Central Depot, New York, on the Harlem Railroad, or forty-five minutes by the Third Avenue and Suburban Elevated Roads, will bring you to Fordham; and less than a hundred paces from either depot are the high iron gates and massive pillars that mark the entrance to Fordham College. To the right of the entrance stands the gate-keeper's lodge, a pretty little cottage of granite and marble set among beds of bright-colored flowers and well-kept plots of grass, and with its pointed gables and narrow windows peeping out from the foliage of the overhanging trees. Straight ahead lies a handsome driveway and, dimly seen through the trees on the right, are the college buildings.

A few yards from the gate the broad drive separates into two avenues which run almost parallel for a short distance and then gradually diverge, one sweeping around to the left, on the edge of a little bluff overlooking the railroad; the other, the approach to the college proper, winding its sinuous way up a gentle incline on the right to the main entrance of the college, and both meeting on the brow of the little hill to complete the circuit of the lawn.

Rows of magnificent elms border both avenues, arching overhead and mingling their branches to cast a welcome shade on the road beneath. What memories do these elms call up in the mind of every old Fordham student! The first objects to greet him coming; the last to wave him a stately farewell. What old student, returning, does not gaze with admiration on their towering forms, their spreading branches, and the high-

bred courtesy with which they seem to bow their welcome.*

Following the road to the right, you pass for fifty
or a hundred yards in a direct line, catching an occasional glimpse of massive granite building or gilded
cross partly seen through the swaying branches, until
an abrupt turn in the avenue brings you at once into
full view of the college buildings. Directly across the
lawn, to the extreme left, stands a square, imposing
structure, furrowed and grizzled by years of exposure,
with its latticed windows, its massive buttresses, and
its unmistakable air of antiquity. It is the building
formerly occupied by St. Joseph's Theological Seminary, but now used as a preparatory school for young
boys, under the name of St. John's Hall. Adjoining
the Hall is the little college church of Our Lady of
Mercy, the use of which has been given to the people
of the vicinity, and whose windows are said to be the
first stained windows ever imported to this country.

Further on to the right you catch the sheen of sun
on a hothouse roof, that peeps up from the green of a
garden half-hidden from view, by that most ancient of
Fordham relics, the infirmary. This is the original
Rose Hill manor house, a plain, old-fashioned two-story
wooden house that had weathered many a storm, and
was drifting into a ripe old age when our republic was
gasping and struggling for its first breath. Further to
the right, and to the rear, the out-buildings, farm-houses,

---

* For many years a tradition has obtained at Fordham that the seed of these
elms was brought from Holyrood Palace, Edinburgh, Scotland, by Lord Stirling, whose daughter, Lady Mary Alexander, the wife of Robert Watts, lived
in the old Rose Hill mansion, now the Infirmary, during the Revolutionary
War. This, however, is not probable, as the trees could not have attained their
present size in that length of time.

THE OLD MANOR HOUSE, WASHINGTON'S HEADQUARTERS.

and servants' quarters are dimly seen, and as your gaze follows the bend in the road it falls full on the main entrance, the central building, the Rose Hill manor house of a later date, with its long brick wings and white observatory, and over whose roof can be seen the towering granite walls of the more modern buildings.

In front of this venerable pile the statue to the founder of the college is erected. On the highest point of the grounds it stands, facing the gate and the opposite hills, with the lawn sloping gracefully down from its pedestal to the railroad bed below.

A hundred yards further up the avenue another turn discloses a group of buildings until now hidden by the trees. Here is the latest instance of the rapid growth of St. John's during recent years, for some of these buildings are almost fresh from the mason's hands. To the right you see the slated roof and tapering chimney of Science Hall; to the left, barely seen over the roofs of intervening houses, is the new Juniors' Hall; and before you, set back a short distance from the roadway, is a tall, imposing structure that has not yet passed from the builder's hands. This is the new Faculty building, and is to contain, besides the rooms of the professors, the students' chapel, and refectories for both the students and the community. Like all the buildings erected since the experiment on the gate-keeper's lodge, it is of granite, faced with marble, with a graceful marble portico shading the entrance. It has four stories and a mansard roof, surmounted by a dome and a twelve-foot cross.

A year ago ground had not been broken for this handsome edifice, and the old First Division building, or Seniors' Hall, with its rough, unfinished wall, was a familiar sight to every visitor at Fordham. The Seniors' Hall was erected in 1865, but the end facing the lawn was kept in a rough, unfinished state, as an extension at that point was contemplated. Something interfered with the plans, however, and for over twenty years that eccentric-looking wall stared in the face of the visitor. The Faculty building joining the Hall at right angles, has at last come to take the place of the long-promised extension, and now the original building is almost entirely hidden from the observer on the lawn.

The interior of the new building is not yet complete, and we can therefore give but a rough description of it. A hallway will connect the entrance with the older building, and the chapel will be at the left or north end. It will occupy the first and second stories for about eighty-three feet. In the southern end on the first and second floors, corresponding to the house of worship, will be the two refectories, and the three stories above will be occupied by the professors.

Passing from the contemplation of this latest addition, beautiful and proud in its new-born strength, twenty paces will bring you to the grizzled front of the main entrance, the grand old building about which the college has grown and developed in the last fifty years. Here is the cradle of Fordham College. Here, in its struggling infancy, it was nursed and tended until it grew beyond the limits of those four massive walls. Built of rough-hewn rock, but built so stoutly and so well as to defy for centuries the onslaughts of wind and storm, this building is a fitting type of him to whose zeal and energy the institution owes its existence. A flight of well-worn marble steps, flanked by two urns filled with flowers and creeping plants, leads up to the broad entrance, and a portico upheld by massive marble pillars adds to the air of imposing grandeur that characterizes the old building.*

Rising above the broad flat roof is the observatory, surmounted by the old clock whose well-known face has recorded the passing of time, day after day, year after year, longer than the oldest Fordhamite can tell, and the familiar notes of whose mournful chime have rung in the ears of Fordham students for the last forty-five years. The old clock came to Fordham in 1846, with the Jesuits from Kentucky. It had come originally from Fribourg, Switzerland, whence it was brought to Amiens, France. In 1841 it was transported to Mount Mary, Kentucky, and then to Fordham in 1846. Many a holy religious long ago laid at rest has responded to its plaintive call to matins or vespers, and many a wrinkled visage smiles on its cold, expressionless face as on the face of an old, familiar friend.

From the steps looking across the lawn a magnificent view is obtained. Directly opposite, Fordham Heights, famous in Revolutionary history, rise, dotted here and there with gabled cottages or bits of dusty road peeping out from the luxuriant foliage, while away in the dim, uncertain distance a thin blue haze marks the course of the far-off Hudson. There, seemingly within a stone's throw, is the little knoll where brooded the gloomy genius of the unhappy Poe. On the edge of a

---

* Until 1885 or 1886, a venerable willow-tree stood opposite the entrance to this building. How long it had stood there no one could tell, but it was old and weather-beaten when the college was opened. It had long stood, dismantled of its branches, and was removed only to avert the danger of its falling.

bluff that commands a view of the surrounding country as far as the sparkling waters of Long Island Sound, in a spot whose poetic surroundings would charm the most obdurate muse, stands the modest little cottage where he lived his sad and fateful life. A short distance back from the old Kingsbridge road that winds up the toilsome ascent of Fordham Heights, it stands, half-hidden among the leaves of a group of apple and cherry trees. Unchanged it stands, as it stood when its unfortunate owner struggled so manfully beneath its roof, for many a long year, with the unrelenting foe to whose attacks he succumbed at last.

But the poetic beauty of this spot is a thing of the past. Mammon now holds sway where once Apollo reigned; that vandal, Modern Improvement, has seized upon that charming bit of Arcadia, and now the sounds of hammer and trowel drown the last sweet plaint of poor Poe's heartbroken muse. Unsightly buildings, beautiful according to the taste of an age of Philistines, now disfigure the once picturesque spot, and unless some generous patron of letters interferes to preserve this last relic, a few years hence will see not a vestige even of the little cottage itself.

But to return to the college. Turning from the contemplation of the magnificent view, you continue the ascent of the marble steps and pass through the wide doorway into the lofty tiled hall. To the right, occupying the entire depth of the building, is the reception-room, a handsome apartment richly furnished and hung with some choice old paintings. On the left are the offices of the president and treasurer, and a broad staircase leading to the Sodality chapel, and connecting with the upper floors of the wings. A pas-

Faculty Building and Seniors' Hall.

sage here leads to the students' refectory, which occupies the ground floor of the north wing.

The refectory is a handsome room about seventy-five feet long, the walls and ceiling frescoed with emblematic and ornamental designs, and lighted by long windows opening at one side on the lawn, at the other on the recreation grounds. The corresponding floor in the south wing is used as a chapel for the students, but will be converted into music rooms as soon as the new chapel is ready for occupation. The floor above, now occupied by the Faculty, will then become the infirmary.

Passing out through the rear door of the old building, you step into a long, narrow extension of three stories containing the music-rooms, the porter's lodge, the wardrobe, and the community library. This extension formerly connected with the old Second Division building, which was torn down last summer. Stepping from the door at the right of this passage (for it is little better than a passage), you find yourself on a spot of ground which has been trodden by the feet of Fordham students more, perhaps, than any other spot on the college grounds.

This was once the old quadrangle, formed by the building just described, the chapel, and an extension that ran at right angles with the latter. Across this little square, generations of students have walked to and from the chapel, the refectory, the parlor, and the offices, and, departing, have given way to others who have followed in their footsteps again and again, and in their turn resigned their places to others.

In the centre of this quadrangle a handsome bronze statue of the Blessed Virgin was erected in 1887 to

commemorate the fiftieth anniversary of the founding
of the Parthenian Sodality.   The sodality is older than
the college, having been organized at Rayville, Ky.,
and come to Fordham with the Jesuits in 1846.

But the quadrangle is no more.   Its sacred precincts
have been invaded by the new building, and its statue
has been relegated to other quarters at the end of the
wardrobe extension, until a suitable site can be found
for it.   The one-story building that formed the southern boundary has disappeared, and, with it, a landmark
that will be missed by many an old Fordhamite.   We
refer to the famous "castle," the mere mention of which
will call up a host of delightful memories in the minds
of the older students.   It was a plain three-story brick
building, joined to the chapel wing by the extension
just described.   It had served successively as a dormitory, office, and class-room building, as a laboratory,
and for several years one floor was utilized as the sanctum sanctorum of the *Fordham Monthly.*   But the
"castle," like the quadrangle, is a thing of the past; it
has gone the way of all bricks and mortar, and now
exists only in the memory of the old-time Fordhamite.

Turning the corner of the partly finished new building, you come in sight of the Seniors' Hall.   It is a
handsome building of four stories and a mansard roof,
and identical in style with the adjoining edifice.   On
the ground floor are the billiard- and reading-rooms of
the senior division, and the gymnasium, which is also
used as a temporary armory and drill-room for the
cadets, and which is furnished with a batting-net for
the winter practice of the baseball team.

On the second story is the study hall.   At the
further end of this room is the stage, whereon many a

SCIENCE HALL.

budding actor has ranted and mouthed and sawed the air, for Fordham has a Dramatic Association almost as old as the college itself.

On the two floors above the study hall are class-rooms and the dormitory, and on the fifth floor, locally known as "Fifth Avenue," are the rooms of the lay members of the Faculty.

Some thirty or forty yards south of the Seniors' Hall is Science Hall, a two-story building with a tall chimney at the end, facing the lawn. This building is devoted almost entirely to the scientific department. On the first floor, to the left of the hall, is the labora-tory of the class in Analytical Chemistry, and a lecture-room for the class of Logic and Metaphysics. Opposite is a handsome, spacious library for the use of the stu-dents, lined with well-filled shelves and furnished with tables, desks, and every facility for study and research. Over the rostrum at the further end is a bas-relief of His Holiness, Leo XIII., and on either side and in adjoining corners are silken banners and pennants, trophies of athletic contests, while the bust of many a learned sage looks down from shelf and pedestal. Here, among these congenial surroundings, the Debat-ing and Historical Societies hold their meetings, and here, with Cicero and Demosthenes looking down on them from their lofty seats and firing their souls with enthusiasm, embryo orators pour forth their elo-quence.

On the upper floor are the lecture-rooms for chemis-try and physics, and the museum, and in the basement are the engine and dynamos that supply heat and light to this great institution ; for it is lighted throughout by electricity and heated by steam. A tunnel connects

the engine-room with all the buildings, and through it
are made all connections for pipe and wire.

Climbing from the murky depths of the engine-room
into the open air, you pass again through the little
group of trees that separates Science Hall from the
Seniors' Hall, and a few steps will bring you to the
edge of the broad, level campus intersected by shady
walks, and with its two baseball diamonds on which
Fordham's representatives in the athletic world have
won so many glorious victories. A cinder-track encir-
cles the First Division field, on which the larger dia-
mond is laid out, and across the field, in the furthest
corner, can be seen through the trees the chute of the
toboggan slide.

Repassing the Seniors' Hall and turning from the
cinder track, you cross a broad, level, though somewhat
dusty, court, sacred to the genius of lawn tennis, to the
Juniors' Hall. This is, in general outline, a counter-
part of its older neighbor, the Seniors', but as it has
yet to complete its first year of existence, it has no
traditions, no memories of bygone days to enhance the
interest of the visitor.

And here you find yourself on the confines of the
garden. Who that has ever visited Fordham can forget
that garden, with its broad boxwood hedges, its glis-
tening walks, and the cool, inviting shade of its arbors?
What student of Fordham can ever forget the noctur-
nal raids on those selfsame arbors, or the stolen ram-
bles amid its hedge-lined walks and shady corners?

A turn in the walk brings us to the rear of the infirmary, the most interesting building on the college
property. The exact date at which this old house was
erected we have no means of ascertaining, but that it

Front Entrance of St. John's Hall, Preparatory Department, Fordham, Showing Junior Cadets.

was old when our forefathers fought the good fight of
a century ago, is an undeniable fact. The old building
has been altered from time to time since it became the
property of the college; wings have been added and
the interior arrangements entirely remodelled, but, in
spite of changes and improvements, it still bears a delightful air of antiquity. Tradition ascribes to this
time-honored relic the distinction of having served
as General Washington's headquarters during some of
the manœuvres preceding the battle of White Plains.
Among the many venerable trees that surround and
overshadow the houses is the identical tree (so says
again infallible tradition) to which the Father of his
Country tied his horse on dismounting. It is believed
by a great many that this old manor house is the building in and about which the principal incidents described
in Fenimore Cooper's novel, "The Spy," took place.

Emerging from the front door of this historic little
house you find yourself once more looking out over the
lawn toward Fordham. To the left, a short distance
away, is the main entrance, and before you, a little to
your right, is the group of venerable trees beneath whose
spreading branches generations of students have delivered their valedictories and received their diplomas.
For the commencement exercises are held in the open
air, a tent being spread under the trees and a temporary
platform erected for the speakers.

And now, turning your steps to the right, after a
brief interval of flagged walk bordered by garden fence
and shrubbery, you come to the most charming spot
in this collection of noble buildings and picturesque
surroundings. St. John's Hall, the preparatory school
for small boys attached to the college, is situated at the

extreme northwest of the college grounds, and farthest of any of the departments from the central building. Adjoining it is the parish church of Fordham, the Church of Our Lady of Mercy. Church and Hall were built in 1845 by Archbishop Hughes, the latter as a seminary for the education of priests for the diocese of New York, and the former as the seminary chapel. Both buildings are of stone quarried on the college property, but different from that used in the other buildings.

The church is a handsome little edifice Gothic in architecture, with its walls and the arches of its ceiling handsomely frescoed and lighted by six magnificent windows. These represent the four evangelists and Saints Peter and Paul.

The Hall is an imposing structure, the massive arched entrance, the old-fashioned latticed windows, the vine-covered walls, all combining to produce an effect at once grand and impressive. The seminary was moved in 1860 to Troy, N. Y., and the buildings sold to the college authorities, for what was a good sum in those days. For a long time the Hall was little used, the classes of Chemistry and Physics alone being held there, but in 1885, under the presidency of Father Dealy, it was thoroughly overhauled and fitted up to fill the requirements of the preparatory school.

In front of it is a small piece of ground, tastefully laid out, shaded by noble trees and cooled by the spray from a handsome fountain, and with gravel walks winding among plots of grass and beds of flowers. From front to rear of the building runs a broad hallway. On either side and on the floors above are the study hall, class-rooms, and dormitories, and in the

St. John's Hall (Preparatory Department), Fordham.

basement are the gymnasium and drill-room. At the rear, fronting the railroad, is the boy's playground. Two handsome terraces, banked with well-kept grass and ornamented with rows of spreading trees shading gravel walks, extend for a distance of fifty yards, and beyond stretches away the level green of the ball-field.

Near the Hall, and also facing the lawn, is a square, one-story stone building which I have hitherto over-looked. It was built in 1840, and in it were lodged the few theological students attending the seminary while the latter was in course of erection. It was af-terward the residence of the parish priest, and has lately been thrown into one large apartment, and is used for the meetings of parish societies.

Running in an easterly direction from the rear of the Hall, is a narrow lane that leads down through the college property, to the woods that border the pictur-esque Bronx, a half-mile away. On one side are the farmyard with its outhouses, the quarters of the ser-vants, and the workshops, and on the other, separated from the lane by a high wall, is the garden, in one cor-ner of which is the little cemetery where so many of the fathers and scholastics, and even some of the stu-dents, sleep their last sleep. In 1890 the cemetery was opened for the reception of the bodies which, until then, had lain in the land sold by the college to the city for the Bronx Park. Passing along this wall and between the skating ponds, the lane crosses the Southern Boule-vard and is lost in the woods until recently the prop-erty of the college, but now forming a portion of Bronx Park, having been purchased by the city for that pur-pose.

Such, then, is the Fordham of to-day.   In fifty years it has risen, in the words of Archbishop Hughes, " from the condition of an unfinished house in a field to the cluster of which it is now composed."   From an ob-scure school in a still more obscure village, it has attained the position of one of the first educational institutions in the country ; and another half-century, it is to be hoped, will find it a flourishing university in the heart of the metropolis of the western hemisphere.

Approach to the "Rose Hill Manor".—The Old College Building.

CHAPTER II.

A MORE pleasing site, or one richer in historic interest, could not have been chosen by Bishop Hughes for his college than this handsome property of Rose Hill, in Westchester County. It is situated in what is, perhaps, the most picturesque part of the county, a region abounding in woodland scenery of infinite variety and unsurpassed beauty. The river Bronx, celebrated in song by that famous Westchester poet, Joseph Rodman Drake, winds its sinuous way through smiling fields and echoing glades, less than half a mile from the college buildings; the wooded sides of Fordham Heights, dotted with cottages, rise over against the college; and away in the distance on either side, as far as the eye can reach, is an ever-changing view of level fields and gently undulating hills.

There is not in all the country a spot so full of historic recollections, teeming as it is with reminiscences of the most thrilling interest. Situated in the heart of the "neutral ground" of revolutionary fame, it has been the scene of many an exciting encounter in those stirring times, when the cannon of the oppressor and the crack of the minute-man's rifle were heard through its valleys, and when "cowboy" and "skinner" roamed through its unprotected settlements, and robbed and pillaged. Nor would we find our interest abated were

2

we to go back to that earlier day, the time of the first
Dutch settlers, or, peering further yet into the hidden
past, to that age when its virgin forests clothed hill
and dale, and sheltered the haunts of the savage Mo-
hegan.   Here, in awful solitude the son of the forest
once sharpened his rude weapons, and kindled his daily
fire, or under the swaying branches took his morning
plunge in the limpid waters of the Bronx.*   Perhaps
on the spot where the college now stands, burned many
a council fire, and tepees clustered where now the seat
of learning rears its walls.

Fordham, with the rest of old Westchester County,
was once a portion of the domain ruled by the chiefs
of the savage tribe of Mohegans.   In 1639, two hundred years before the purchase of the Rose Hill estate
by Bishop Hughes, three Indian sachems, Fecquemeck,
Rechgawac, and Packanarieus, sold to the Dutch West
India Company the lands of Kekesheik, which included
all the land between the Bronx and the Harlem, and
as far north as the present city of Yonkers.   Seven
years later that portion which is now known as Fordham, together with the "Yoncker's land," then known
as Colen Donck, was sold to a young Dutchman named
Adrian Van der Donck.   How long Mynheer Van der
Donck enjoyed his vast property we have no means of
ascertaining, but the records show that some few years
later his widow, Mary, who had in the meantime married Hugh O'Neale, of Patuxent, Md., conveyed the
property to her brother, Elias Doughty, of Flushing, L.
I. Mr. Doughty, in turn, sold the land to John Archer

---

* On the bank of the Bronx, near what was lately the college property, is a
large rock, hollowed out apparently by human handiwork, which tradition '
declares was the bathing place of the early savage.

in 1667. The deed is not a remarkable document, and is not likely to be of much interest to the average reader, but the confirmation of the sale by the Indian chiefs, from the quaintness of its style and its many peculiarities, is, we think, worthy of a place here, and we therefore insert it in full.

Indian Confirmation to John Archer.

Be it known unto all men by these p'sents that upon ye 28th day of Sept. in the 21st year of ye Reigne of our Sovereigne Lord Charles the Second by ye Grace of God of England, Scotland, France and Ireland, King Defend^r of the faith, &c., Anno Domini 1669, we Tacharetht, Mometaihatim Wackha, Pimekekeh, for and on ye behalfe of Ahwaroch, Achipor Maniquaes, Sachemacke, for & in ye behalfe of Annetic Pownocke, for & on ye behalfe of Lyssie, & we on ye behalfe of ye rest of ye owners, for the consideration hereafter expressed have graunted, bargained & sould, & by these p'sents do hereby grant, bargaine and sell unto John Archer, of Fordham, his heirs and assignes, a certaine Tract of upland and meadow ground upon ye maine, beginning Westward from a certaine place by ye Indians comonly called Muscota, so it goes to another place called by them Gowahasuasing & from thence round about ye kill called Papiriniman, & so to rune into Harlem Ryver at ye Hook called Saperewack, from thence it reacheth South East to ye place called Achquechgenom, and from thence it reacheth alongst Bronck's * Ryver to Cowangough, so on to Sachkerah, and so to the first place Muscota, so that from Muscota to Sackerath it runs upon a straight east lyne to Bronck's Ryver & from Saperewack to Achquechgenom, South East by ye said ryver all w^{eh} tract of land, as is before described here, the aforesaid Indians on the behalfe of ourselves, those that have entrusted us and our associates have sould unto ye said John Archer his heirs & assignes for & in consid. of 13 coats of Duffells, one halfe anchor of Rume, 2 cans of Brandy, wine wth several other small matters to ye value of 60 guilders wampum. All which we acknowledge to have received of

---

* This name is spelled variously : Broux, Brunx, Bronck's, Bronk's, Brunck's or Bronkx. Bronx is now the accepted spelling.

him the said John Archer before the ensealing & delivery of these pr'sents in full satisfaction for ye land afore men. Comed the w^{ᵒʰ} we doe hereby resigne and make over unto ye s^d John Archer, his heirs and assignes w^{ᵗʰ} all our right title and interest thereunto, as also those that have entrusted any of us o'ʳ & associates to have & to hould the s^d tract of land and premises unto ye s^d John Archer, his heirs & assignes unto ye proper use and behoofe of him ye s^d John Archer, his heirs & assignes forever, free quit, and cleare from all and any form of bargaine & sale, or any other incumbrances by us or by any from or under us & to ye utmost of o'ʳ powers shall keep and save him the s^d John Archer his heirs & assignes, harmlesse in his or their quiett possession & enjoyment of ye premises against any other Indian pr'tenders whatsoever. In witness whereof we have hereunto put o'ʳ hand & seales, ye day & yeare first within wrytten.

This bargain & sale was made by ye approbation & lycense of his Hon^{ʳˢ} ye governors between ye partyes mentioned, with this Proviso that his Royall Highness, his Rights & Privileges as Lord Proprietor of these his territoryes be hereby not any infringed.

MATTHIAS NICHOLLS, Sec^r,

Entered by JOHN ARCHER,*
March 4, 1669.

Four years after the transfer of this land by Elias Doughty, Governor Francis Lovelace issued letters patent granting to John Archer the manor of Fordham. The new manor is described in this document, as "upon the main continent, situate, lying and being to the Eastward of Harlem River, near unto ye passage commonly called *Spiting Devil*, upon which ye *New Dorp or Village is erected*, known by the *name of Fordham*." † This is signed by Francis Lovelace, and

* Albany Deed Book, vol. iii., pp. 127, 128.
† Albany Record, vol. xxiii., 26–52.

bears also the signatures of Michael Bastyensen and Valentyn Claessen. This is the first time the name of Fordham appears on the records of Westchester County.* The original village did not occupy the present site, but was situated at a point farther west, on the bank of the Harlem. Farmer's Bridge now crosses the river at this point, connecting the mainland with Manhattan Island, and near by is the village of Kingsbridge.

· A few years after the granting of the manor of Fordham, the little village was stirred up by an incident which, from certain peculiar features, is not without significance to those who have observed the steady growth of the Catholic Church in America, and the increasing tendency toward religious toleration on the part of our Protestant neighbors. It is recorded in the annals of the early colonial government, that in October, 1673, on the restoration of the Dutch rule, the people of the village of Fordham, through Mynheer Cornelius Steenwyck, presented a petition to the Governor asking that they be released from what they termed the tyrannous rule of Archer, and be permitted to elect their own magistrate. An investigation followed and Archer freely consented to the change, whereupon the following decree was issued :

The inhabitants of the town of Fordham are hereby authorized to nominate by a plurality of the votes of their town, six of the best qualified persons, *exclusively of the Reformed Christian Religion,* as magistrates of said town, and to present said nomination by the first opportunity to the Governor-General, from which his Honor will then make the selection ; it is also recommended them

* The name of Fordham is derived from two Saxon words, *foord* (a ford) and *ham* (a mansion).

to pay attention when nominating, that the half, at least, of those nominated, be of the Dutch nation.

Dated, New Harlem, 4th of Oct. 1673.*

According to this decree the candidates were to be of "the Reformed Christian religion" only. No other would be tolerated, and a Catholic candidate was a thing unheard of. They would as soon admit a Catholic to a share in the government as erect a statue of Brahma or Isis in their meeting-house. The Catholic was ignored, tabooed, and excluded from a share in the rights and privileges accorded to his fellow-colonists. And yet two hundred years later we find that very town the seat of an institution for the diffusion of Catholic doctrine, and the obscure little village, then scarcely known or heard of outside of its own narrow precincts, is blazoned throughout the land as the home of one of the foremost Catholic colleges of the country, reflecting some of the glory and renown it could never hope to attain through its own merits.

But to return to the history of the town. John Archer had, under date of September 18, 1669, mortgaged his lands for 2,200 guilders seawant, to Cornelius Steenwyck, a merchant of New York, the same whose name appears in connection with the petition for the change of government at Fordham; and on November 14, 1671, he gave a second mortgage for 7,000 guilders. In October, 1685, John Archer was found dead in his coach while on his way from Fordham to New York, and the same month his son, John Archer, Jr., transferred the entire estate to Cornelius Steenwyck and Margaretta, his wife.

In due time Mynheer Steenwyck went the way of all

* New York Col. MSS., vol. ii., p. 625.

flesh, and his widow married Dominie Henricus Selyns. January 10, 1694, they conveyed to "Colonel Nicholas Bayard, Captain Isaac Vermilyea, Jacob Bolen Rockloyzun, and John Harpendinck, then elders and overseers of the Nether Dutch Church within the city of New York, and their lawful successors and heirs and posterity, the said manor of Fordham lying in the county of Westchester."

About this time, or several years before, the Fordham manor was parcelled out into several farms, and that portion which is now the college property came into the possession of the Corsa or Corser family. This farm was known as Rose Hill, a name which still clings to the old place, and by which the college was known in its earlier years. The old Rose Hill manor-house is still standing, and is used as the college infirmary. The exact date of the erection of this ancient building is not known, but it is certain that it was standing as early as 1692, for it is recorded that in that year Benjamin Fletcher Corsa was born there.* The Corsa family owes its chief celebrity to the achievements, during the revolutionary war, of Andrew Corsa, the grandson of Benjamin Fletcher Corsa, and the last of the famous Westchester Guides.

This unique corps was composed of a select body of men to whom every foot of the "neutral ground" was familiar, men of tried and proven courage and devotion to the cause of liberty. They lent valuable assistance to the soldiers of the American army, and on more than one occasion proved themselves worthy of recognition. Andrew Corsa was the youngest of these sturdy patriots, and was born in the old homestead January 24,

* Bolton's History of Westchester County.

1762. His father, Captain Isaac Corsa, had served in the British army against the French and Indians, and, like so many of the people of Westchester County, sympathized with the English government. Notwithstanding his father's pronounced views, young Corsa decided to espouse the cause of liberty, and joined the Westchester Guides. He died November 21, 1852, at the ripe old age of ninety.

From about the birth of Andrew Corsa, in 1762, until 1787, the ownership of Rose Hill is enshrouded in mystery. There is no record of its sale by the Corsas until 1787, when it was bought at auction by John Watts and his wife Jane, from Benjamin Corsa. An obituary notice of Andrew Corsa, which appeared in the *Westchester Herald,* says that, at the close of the war, he was obliged to " part with his father's land by compulsory sale." But the purchase of the property was from Benjamin Corsa. The grandfather of Andrew Corsa was Benjamin Fletcher Corsa, and it is possible that he was alive, though at a very advanced age at the time, and that, being a royalist, his property was confiscated and sold at auction. There is a tradition that the estate was confiscated about this time.

The manor-house, however, was not occupied by the Corsa family for many years previous to the sale to John Watts. They certainly lived in it in 1762, for Andrew Corsa was born there in that year, but, between that and 1768, they, for some unknown reason, vacated it. This is known from the fact that John De Lancey, *of Rose Hill*, West Farms, was burgess of the borough of Westchester in the Assembly from 1768 to 1772. He must have relinquished Rose Hill shortly after this, for during the Revolution it was the residence of Robert Watts and his wife, Lady Mary Alexander, daughter of Major-General Lord Stirling, of the American army.* What relationship Robert Watts bore to John Watts, the subsequent purchaser of Rose Hill, does not appear, although it is more than probable that they were of the one family.

John De Lancey, to whom we have alluded as a quondam occupant of Rose Hill, was a grandson of Etienne De Lanci, a Huguenot who left France in 1686 and came to America.† Another grandson, and a brother of John De Lancey, was the famous Colonel James De Lancey, who distinguished himself during the revolutionary war by his activity in behalf of the British government. All of his family, with one or two exceptions, were staunch royalists, but he was preeminent among them for his bitter opposition to the cause of the colonists. He organized the Royal Refugee Corps, or the "Cowboys," as they were frequently called. He kept a recruiting officer constantly at Mile Square, between Fordham and West Farms, and the outrages perpetrated by his followers on the inhabitants of the "neutral ground" earned for him the hatred and enmity of almost every resident of Westchester County.

At the close of the war the commonwealth of New York, by a formal act of Legislature, withdrew from him her protection, declared his estate, real and personal, forfeit to the people, banished him forever, and, in case of his return to the State at any future time, declared him thereby guilty of felony, and sentenced

* Bolton's History of Westchester County.
† On arriving in England, on his way to America, he Anglicized his name, becoming Stephen De Lancey. Scharf's History of Westchester County.

him to death without the benefit of clergy. So cordially was he hated by his neighbors, for his many acts of depredation, that, as soon as peace was declared, several individual efforts were made to seize his person and prevent him from leaving the country.* His brother, John, was more fortunate than he, for although both were active Tory partisans, the property of James, as we have seen, was confiscated, whereas that of John was not.† Colonel James De Lancey emigrated to Nova Scotia.

The Watts family, into whose possession Rose Hill passed after the Revolution, was closely connected by intermarriages with the De Lanceys. The Honorable John Watts, probably the father of Colonel John Watts who purchased Rose Hill, and perhaps also of Robert Watts, was married to a sister of Lieutenant-Governor De Lancey. Colonel John Watts, afterward of Rose Hill, was married to his cousin, Jane De Lancey, sister of John and the notorious Colonel James De Lancey. In 1774 he was appointed Royal Recorder of the city of New York, and was the last to hold that office. From 1791 to 1798 he was Speaker in the Assembly of New York, and afterward became a Member of Congress. He was the first judge of the Court of Common Pleas in Westchester County, serving from 1802 to 1807.‡

There is a tradition fondly cherished at Fordham that General Washington was, on more than one occasion, an honored guest at the Rose Hill manor-house. There is no doubt that General Washington frequently passed through that district while reconnoitring the

* Historical Magazine, November, 1862.
† Scharf's History of Westchester County.   ‡ Ibid.

WALK SKIRTING COLLEGE CAMPUS, FORDHAM.

passes and defiles between Throgg's Neck, where the British had effected a landing in the autumn of 1776, and Fordham Heights. On one occasion, early in October, 1776, he rode over from Kingsbridge to Westchester Village, late in the afternoon,* and on the 14th of the same month, " accompanied by the generals of the army who were at headquarters, he visited all the posts beyond Kingsbridge and the several passes and roadways which led from Throgg's Neck, acquainting himself, as far as he could by personal reconnoissance, with the character and condition of the outlets from Throgg's Neck." †

While on some of these frequent excursions, it is believed, he sojourned at the Rose Hill mansion. And the belief is certainly well founded, for, in the first place, General Stirling, the father-in-law of the tenant of Rose Hill, was at that time with the army on Fordham Heights, so that, if the Commander-in-chief stopped by the way, it is more than probable that he accepted the hospitality of such avowed sympathizers with the cause over whose destinies he presided. Moreover, the only roads by which he could go from the Heights to Throgg's Neck, were the Kingsbridge road, which now passes close to the college gate, and the Kingsbridge and Williamsbridge road, which lies a mile to the north of the college, either of which was within a short distance of the Rose Hill mansion.

Another tradition of revolutionary days, but one which lacks the color of probability, is that concerning the skeletons which were discovered in a mound at the rear of the old seminary. They were immediately pronounced the bones of soldiers who had fallen in

* Scharf's History of Westchester County.　　　　† Ibid.

some of the numerous skirmishes that took place in
that vicinity during the revolutionary war.   But there
is nothing to confirm that belief ; on the contrary, all
the evidence in the case tends to contradict any such
opinion.   The skeletons were buried at regular intervals and in regular order, which would hardly be the
case with those dying on a battlefield ; there were no
tokens, in the way of brass buttons, buckles, sabres
and the like, such as would, in all probability, be found
in the graves of soldiers; and finally, at the time the
bones were discovered, a Mr. Corsa, who lived in the
neighborhood, stated, it is said, that the place had been
used in former years as a burying-ground.

We have already told how Rose Hill passed finally into the possession of the Watts family.   It was
bought at auction for £530, by Colonel John Watts,
who afterward transferred it to Robert Watts.   The
latter, in his will, dated January 23, 1814, bequeathed
it to his son, Robert Watts, Jr., who, ten years later,
sold it to Henry Barclay, a nephew of John and James
De Lancey.   From him the estate passed to Warren
De Lancey, and thence through the hands of several
owners to Elias Brevoort, who in 1836 sold it to
Horatio Shephard Moat, of Kings County.   In 1838
Mr. Moat built the stone house which is now the
central building of the college, and in which are the
principal offices and the reception-room.   Through Mr.
Andrew Carrigan, the new house, with a farm of
ninety-eight acres, was purchased, in 1839, by Bishop
Hughes, for $30,000.   It cost $10,000 more to fit the
place to meet the requirements of an educational institution, and on June 24, 1841, the feast of St. John
the Baptist, under whose patronage the institution was

placed, the college was formally opened. Reverend John McCloskey, afterward Archbishop of New York, and the first American to wear the cardinal's hat, was installed as president. The following September studies were commenced. The names of six students were entered on the rolls, and the nucleus of the present grand institution was firmly established.

CHAPTER III.

ARCHBISHOP HUGHES.

IT would seem but meagre recognition of the services of Archbishop Hughes in the cause of Catholicity, but more especially of Catholic education, were we to dismiss him, in this work, with a mere occasional mention. In admiring the beauty of the handiwork, we must not lose sight of the hand that wrought it or the mind that guided that hand. Therefore a little space devoted to a biographical sketch of the illustrious prelate will not be out of place.

John Hughes was born on June 24, the feast of St. John the Baptist, 1797, at Annaloghan, near Augher, County Tyrone, Ireland. His father, Patrick Hughes, was a small farmer, who, although in comfortable circumstances, and able to provide well for his large family, was by no means affluent or wealthy. A staunch Catholic, he faithfully performed his duty to God and man, even under circumstances most trying and unfavorable, and at a time when his native country was groaning under the weight of the penal laws. Young John, who was the third of a family of seven, received his early education at a little school in Augher, and later attended the high school at Auchnacloss. From his earliest childhood he evinced a strong desire for the priesthood. "Many a time," said he in later life, "have I thrown down my rake in the

ARCHBISHOP HUGHES,
FOUNDER OF THE COLLEGE.

meadow, and kneeling behind a hayrick, begged of God and the Blessed Virgin to let me become a priest." He early displayed an aptitude for learning and a fondness for his books that gave promise of a brilliant future. But the plans of the young student and his fond parents were destined to be thwarted, and their dreams of the future rudely dispelled. By a train of untoward circumstances, his career at school was brought to an untimely end, and his hopes for a time completely shattered.

The rude awakening from the gilded dreams of youth, and the subsequent reverses that prevented him from resuming his beloved studies, must seem to the casual observer to be most unfortunate ; but when we look back now and review his eventful life and the various influences that went to shape his course, we cannot but feel that his very misfortunes were providential; we cannot but see the hand of God guiding him, by means of those very misfortunes, to the field of labor that was awaiting him in another land.

When he had reached the age of eighteen, his father's repeated losses and consequent reduced circumstances forced John to leave school. Sad indeed was the parting of the studious boy from the books which he loved so well, and bitter was the thought of resigning the career that his sanguine mind had already mapped out for himself. But his father's needs were pressing and the call of duty was imperative, so he laid aside the book and the pen to follow the plough and wield the pick. But he did not give up hope. His evenings, his holidays (what few he had), his every spare moment were devoted to his studies, and though his progress was slow his enthusiasm was no whit abated.

It was soon made evident that he would never become a successful farmer. He could not adapt himself to the calling, and he saw that it was folly to continue to apply himself to such uncongenial work. Therefore his father placed him with a friend of the family, who was gardener at Favor Royal, the family seat of the Moutrays, situate near the farm of Patrick Hughes. There the young man was to pursue the study of horticulture. There, as when he worked at home, his every spare moment was devoted to his books, and hours were stolen from his rest that he might give them to study.

Strange as it may seem, study or the acquisition of knowledge was not the end for which he strove. His was not the nature of a scholar, a nature which followed learning for learning's sake. "He was a man of action rather than a man of study, and probably under no circumstances would he have become a profound scholar. But a certain amount of scholarship was a necessary qualification for the priesthood, and having made up his mind to be a priest in spite of all obstacles, he shrank from no labor which brought him nearer to his object." *

During all this time the affairs of the Hughes family were becoming steadily more complicated. One misfortune followed another, until at last they decided to emigrate to America, whither so many of their fellow-countrymen had preceded them. Accordingly, in 1816, with his second son, Patrick, the father sailed for Baltimore, Md., and arriving there, proceeded to Chambersburg, Franklin County, Pa., where he eventually settled. A year later the subject of this brief biography followed, and after spending a short time

* Hassard's Life of Archbishop Hughes.

with his father at Chambersburg, returned to Baltimore, where his brother, in the meantime, had obtained work. There he, too, secured employment, under a gardener, with whom he worked until the approach of winter rendered his further services there unnecessary, and he was obliged to look elsewhere for employment. He retraced his steps to Chambersburg, and there for a year or more worked at anything that offered—in the quarries, digging ditches, making roads, or anything else by which he could earn an honest dollar. In August, 1818, the rest of the family arrived from Ireland and settled in Chambersburg, where, by that time, the father had acquired considerable means.

But during all this time young John had not relinquished for a moment his desire to enter the priesthood. He still fondly cherished the hope of finishing his studies, and, as in Ireland, every spare moment was devoted to his books. He had applied, again and again, for admission to Mount St. Mary's College at Emmettsburg, Md., but his efforts met with failure. He had no money, but was willing to give his services in any capacity in return for his education. But there was no vacancy for him, and all his efforts were in vain.

In the latter part of 1818, or the early months of the following year, he started for Emmettsburg, determined to obtain work in the village, and be on the spot to seize the first opportunity that offered to gain admission to the college. He worked about Emmettsburg until November, 1819, when the long looked-for opportunity arrived. At this time there chanced to be a vacancy in the garden, and young Hughes, relying

3

on his experience at Favor Royal, and later at Baltimore, immediately applied for the position. He was
accepted, and an agreement was entered into between
him and Father Dubois,* by which, in return for his
services, he would receive private instruction until
such time as he would be sufficiently proficient to
enter the regular classes and teach the younger pupils.
Here, then, at last, was the reward for which he had
labored and struggled through all these years; the
goal was almost reached, the dreams and ambitions of
a lifetime were about to be realized.

It is marvellous to note how the chain of circumstances, beginning with the first of his father's reverses,
seems to lead up to this important event, and that the
very work to which necessity obliged him to turn on
leaving school should afterward prove the means of
his entering on the career which Almighty God had reserved for him in the New World. Commenting on this,
his biographer, Mr. Hassard, says: "In the toilsome
paths by which he had been led to this spot, how plain-
ly do we not see the hand of God!   Had not pecuniary
losses compelled his father to take him away from
school, he might have lived and died a parish priest in
Ireland. He would have been distinguished, it is true,
but distinction supposes opportunity as well as talent,
and Ireland afforded no field for the full display of his
peculiar powers. And again, had not necessity compelled him, much against his inclination, to dig, water,
and weed at Favor Royal, though we cannot doubt
that he would have found some way of getting into the
priesthood—for he generally did whatever he determined
to do—he might not have got admission to Mount St.

* Afterward Bishop of New York.

Mary's College; he might never have known either Mr. Dubois, or his associate, Father Bruté—both of whom exerted a happy influence upon his early career; and so the whole current of his life might have been changed."

He spent about nine months working in the garden at Mount St. Mary's, and having attracted the attention of Father Dubois by his diligence and the progress he had made, he was admitted as a regular student, at the Fall term of the following year. As we have already remarked, he was not endowed with the attributes that mark the profound scholar. In the studies of rhetoric and polite literature he never became distinguished, and it was not until he took up philosophy and theology that all his strength and power of mind were displayed to advantage. He was ordained deacon in 1825, and about a year later, October 15, 1826, he was elevated to the priesthood by Bishop Conwell, of Philadelphia, at St. Joseph's Church, in that city. Within the same month his old friend and patron, Father Dubois, was consecrated Bishop of New York at the cathedral in Baltimore.

The newly ordained priest was assigned to the mission of Bedford, then a wild, rough district in the western part of Pennsylvania, but two years later he was called to Philadelphia. The diocese at that time was in a state bordering almost on disruption, owing to disputes over the wretched trustee system of church government, and the bishop was in a constant state of strife with both clergy and laity. From the first Father Hughes was a bitter opponent of the system, and he lost no opportunity to express his disapproval, both by word and deed. Its final overthrow in Philadelphia was due in no small measure to his efforts, and when he was placed in charge of the New York diocese one of his first acts was to have it completely crushed out of existence. During the ten years he spent in Philadelphia he had ample opportunity to indulge his propensity for controversy, an occupation for which he was peculiarly fitted. He engaged in many bitter disputes with prominent Protestant divines, and soon gained renown for the vigor and energy with which he entered into these tilts, and the triumph which inevitably crowned his efforts.

In the fall of 1829, when the question arose of appointing an administrator of the diocese of Philadelphia, and a probable successor to Bishop Conwell, who was then unable to perform the arduous duties of that office, the bishop recommended Father Hughes to the Holy See, as a man eminently fitted for the position. The recommendation, however, had no effect, and the Reverend Francis P. Kenrick, President of the Theological Seminary at Bardstown, Ky., was chosen instead. In 1833, while he was deep in his famous controversy with the Reverend Mr. Breckenridge, he and the Reverend John B. Purcell were nominated for the bishopric of Cincinnati. Again he was set aside and the other nominee appointed, but through a most extraordinary circumstance—a circumstance which seems only to confirm one in the belief that Almighty God was reserving him for a greater work. Bishop England, who was then at Rome, had had several interviews with the Cardinal Prefect of the Propaganda on the subject of this appointment, and one day the latter said: "There are two candidates, bishop, between whom the Sacred Congregation is utterly at a loss how to decide; these are the Reverend John Hughes and the Reverend John B. Purcell. If you can mention any particular, no matter how trifling, in which one seems to you better qualified than the other, I think a decision may be reached at once."

The bishop hesitated, for he was really perplexed. At last he answered:

"There is one point, your Eminence, which may deserve to be considered. Mr. Hughes is emphatically a self-made man, and perhaps he would be on that account more acceptable to the people of a Western diocese than Mr. Purcell."

"Ah!" said the cardinal, "I think that will do."

The next day he met Bishop England again, and exclaimed with an air of satisfaction:

"Well, bishop, the question is settled. As soon as I told the cardinals what you said about *Mr. Purcell's* being a self-made man, they agreed upon him unanimously, and the nomination will at once be presented to his Holiness for approval."

"I was about to explain the mistake," said Bishop England, afterward, "but I reflected that it was no doubt the work of the Spirit of God, and was silent."

The cardinal never knew of his blunder.* To us, looking back now on the subsequent career of this great man, how full of meaning must Bishop England's remark seem. The sequel has demonstrated, beyond doubt, that it was indeed the work of the Holy Spirit of God. Father Hughes was destined for other work.

In 1835 the appointment of several new bishops became necessary. The growth of the Philadelphia diocese called for the erection of a new see at Pittsburgh,

* Hassard's Life of Archbishop Hughes.

and the failing health of Bishop Dubois, of New York, necessitated the selection of a coadjutor. Bishop Kenrick was appointed to the see of Pittsburgh, declining an invitation from Bishop Dubois to become the latter's coadjutor, and Father Hughes was appointed to succeed him as coadjutor to Bishop Conwell, whose mind had become affected by old age. Complications arose, however, which prevented these appointments from going into effect until the next council of Baltimore.

The council met on April 16, 1837, and it was decided then that the diocese of Philadelphia should remain intact, and Father Hughes was appointed coadjutor to Bishop Dubois. On November 3d, he received formal notice that he had been chosen. The scene in his church, when he announced his intention of accepting the appointment, is described by the historian as affecting in the extreme. On January 2, 1838, he departed for the scene of his future labors, and it is recorded of him that he refused several invitations from prominent and wealthy people to pass the evening before his departure with them, to spend it with an humble friend whom he had met while a day-laborer at Emmittsburg.*

On January 8th, at the Cathedral of St. Patrick, Mott Street, New York, he was consecrated bishop of Basileopolis, *in partibus infidelium*, and coadjutor to the Bishop of New York. The ceremony was performed by Bishop Dubois, assisted by Bishop Kenrick and Bishop Fenwick, of Boston, and the sermon was preached by Father Mulledy, the distinguished Jesuit. The cathedral was crowded to the doors, and masses

* Hassard's Life of Archbishop Hughes.

of people filled the windows, and swarmed over the platforms which had been erected in the yard.

Two weeks after the consecration of Bishop Hughes, Bishop Dubois was prostrated by an attack of paralysis. A second and a third followed, and so completely shattered the already feeble health of the venerable prelate, that the full burden of the management of the diocese fell on the shoulders of the young coadjutor. But it fell on broad, sturdy shoulders, and he soon proved his entire fitness for the arduous task imposed upon him.

And soon the young bishop found that the task that had fallen to his lot was no easy one, and that the road he was to travel was not a broad and level one, by any means. The diocese comprised a Catholic population of about two hundred thousand, scattered over an area of fifty-five thousand square miles. To minister to the spiritual wants of these people, there were but forty priests, and the number of churches did not exceed twenty. The churches were overwhelmed with debt, and completely under the control of lay trustees. The act which first drew all eyes on Bishop Hughes, and gave the first indication of the vigorous rule which he intended to establish in the diocese, was the battle with, and final subjugation of, that crying evil in church management, lay trusteeism. He had shown himself a vigorous opponent of the system in Philadelphia, and his treatment of it in New York was in perfect keeping with his former conduct.

The abuses to which the system gave rise became almost intolerable, and shortly after the young coadjutor's arrival an incident occurred, which is a fitting example of the insolence bred by such a condition of affairs. The case was rendered the more notable from the fact that it gave Bishop Hughes an opportunity to strike the first decisive blow at the whole system. A priest, who had been attached to the cathedral, was suspended by Bishop Dubois for some act of insubordination, but was reinstated by the trustees, elected rector of the parochial school, and voted a salary, the trustees refusing to recognize the pastor appointed in his stead. They employed a constable to eject from the school a teacher sent there by the bishop, and even threatened to cut off the latter's salary.

Bishop Hughes's treatment of the matter was in every way characteristic of him. "He felt that the battle must be a decisive one," says Mr. Hassard; "it was not an affair of the appointment of school teachers or the payment of salaries; it was practically the question whether the church should be governed by the bishop or the legislature. If the charter of incorporation could give laymen the right of interference when the bishop deemed it necessary to inflict canonical censures upon one of his clergy; if it entitled them to appoint catechists and expel from the premises anybody who did not please them; why might it not go further, and commit to the trustees the entire management of the spiritual concerns of the congregation? If they might demand the services of a suspended priest, why not of an excommunicated priest? Of a Methodist minister? A Jew? A pagan? An atheist? The trustees, in fine, were acting on the Protestant principle, which puts all church matters into the hands of the people; they may call whom they please to preach to them, and if they do not like him, may send him away and call another. The Catholic principle supposes that pastors are sent by God to teach and govern their flocks."

The Sunday following the ejection of the teacher, he spoke from the pulpit on the subject in a quiet manner, and in such a way as to invite an apology from the trustees, and bring about an amicable settlement of the difficulties. As they made no advances he read, on the following Sunday, a vigorous pastoral, which, though signed by Bishop Dubois, was written by himself. It threatened them with the direst ecclesiastical penalties if they persisted in their conduct. It told them that, although, according to the civil law, they could control the building and revenues, they could not control the clergy or the sacraments. They might do what they pleased with the building, but unless they acted in perfect conformity with the canons and spirit of the Catholic church, the priests would all be withdrawn and the cathedral placed under an interdict. The people upheld the bishop in his determined action, and a fatal blow was struck at the system.* His manner of dealing with cases in other parts of the diocese is tersely described in the following note, made by his secretary some years later :

The Archbishop went to —— to give the trustees of St. ——'s a blowing up. The only way will be to blow them out of the church entirely.——N.B.—He turned them out.

This evil rooted out, he turned his attention to a subject which had always been uppermost in his mind —education. Bishop Dubois had attempted, several

---

* An amendment to the civil law, which has since been passed, provides that the trustees of a Catholic church shall be the bishop, the vicar-general, the pastor, and two laymen.

years before, to found a college at Nyack, on the Hudson, but just as the buildings were almost completed they were entirely destroyed by fire. He then thought of transferring the institution to Brooklyn, but this idea was abandoned, and the scheme temporarily dropped. After the arrival of Bishop Hughes a theological seminary and school for secular education was established at Lafargeville, Jefferson County, N. Y., being opened on September 30, 1838, under the patronage of St. Vincent de Paul. But the college was not a success. It was three hundred miles from New York City, and the attendance was so poor that it proved anything but a profitable venture. After considerable search for another site Bishop Hughes came upon the old Rose Hill farm, at Fordham, then in Westchester County. To his mind it was an ideal site. The quiet and seclusion, so conducive to study and meditation, the beauty of the surrounding country, the healthy situation, all seemed to fit the place in a special manner for the end he had in view, and his decision was soon reached. Through Mr. Andrew Carrigan, he purchased the estate with money raised chiefly by voluntary subscriptions throughout the diocese and in Europe. As already told, the college was formally opened on June 24, 1841, under the patronage of St. John the Baptist. The same year the theological seminary was moved from Lafargeville and also established at Fordham, under the patronage of St. Joseph. On October 14, 1841, in a pastoral letter he commended the new college to the liberality of his people, and at the same time announced that Bishop Dubois had resigned the administration of the diocese, owing to his extreme age and ill health. Five years later, in April, 1846, St. John's was raised by the Legislature to the dignity of a university, and placed by Bishop Hughes in the hands of the Jesuit fathers, who came from Kentucky to take charge of it, and under whose direction it has remained ever since.

From 1840 to 1842 another phase of the educational question claimed the attention of Bishop Hughes. This was the Public School question, from the fight over which he came out so gloriously victorious. His movements were directed against the Public School Society, a private corporation which had the entire management of the public schools of New York. This organization disbursed the funds provided by the city for the maintenance of the schools, chose the books to be used, and regulated the entire working of the system. The text-books used teemed with the usual falsehoods and calumnies against Catholicity, the instructors were thoroughly imbued with the anti-Catholic spirit of the age, and the city schools were practically turned into proselytizing institutions of the most flagrant kind. The bishop, however, entered the lists and fought the Public School Society for two years; he fought it through the press, on the platform, and in the halls of the Legislature, and was rewarded in the end by the complete overthrow of the Society, and the establishment of the present system, which, defective as it is, is infinitely superior to that followed under the former *régime.*

It was in 1844, however, that the bishop's strength of character was put to its greatest test. The Know-Nothing movement had been agitating the country for nearly ten years, and had increased in strength and bit-

terness, and finally culminated in the fearful scenes
that were enacted in Philadelphia, on May 8, 1844.
On that day St. Michael's Church, the house of the Sisters of Charity, the church and rectory of St. Augus-
tine, were all burned by the infuriated mob, and the
magnificent library of the Augustinians looted, and
the books committed to the flames.

A committee from the leaders of the Philadelphia
riot immediately started for New York, and a grand
mass meeting of "Native Americans" was called in the
City Hall Park to receive and welcome them.   But
Bishop Hughes was not a man to be dismayed even by
the prospect of a repetition of the Philadelphia outrages.   He warned the enemies of Catholicity, in plain
unmistakable terms, against any attempt to molest the
property of the church.   "If a single Catholic church
were burned in New York," said he, on one occasion,
"the city would become a second Moscow."   In an extra edition of the *Freeman's Journal*, then under his
control, he warned Catholics not to attend any public
meetings, and to avoid especially the meeting in City
Hall Park.   He then called upon Mayor Robert H.
Morris, and advised him to prevent this demonstration.

"Are you afraid," asked the Mayor, "that some of·
your churches will be burned ? "

"No, sir; but I am afraid that some of *yours* will
be burned.   We can protect our own.   I come to warn
you for your own good."

"Do you think, bishop, that your people would attack the procession ? "

"I do not; but the Native Americans want to pro-
voke a Catholic riot, and if they can do it in no other
way, I believe they would not scruple to attack the

procession themselves, for the sake of making it appear that the Catholics had assailed them."

"What, then, would you have me do?"

"I did not come to tell you what to do. I am a churchman, not the mayor of New York; but, if I were the mayor, I would examine the laws of the State, and see if there were not attached to the police force a battery of artillery, a company or so of infantry, and a squadron of horse; and I think I should find that there were; and if so, I should call them out. Moreover, I should send to Mr. Harper, the mayor-elect, who has been chosen by the votes of this party. I should remind him that these men are his supporters; I should warn him that if they carry out their design there will be a riot; and I should urge him to use his influence in preventing this public reception of the delegates."

How far the mayor may have been influenced by this conversation we do not pretend to say, but there was no demonstration on the arrival of the Philadelphia Native Americans, and no disturbance in New York either at this time or when the riots broke out again in Philadelphia in July. The bishop publicly claimed the merit of having prevented an outbreak.*

The continual strain on both mind and body was already beginning to tell on Bishop Hughes. Only such a powerful frame and naturally rugged constitution as his could bear the terrible strain to which he had been subjected for so many years. His health began to fail, and in February, 1844, the Rev. Dr. McCloskey was consecrated his coadjutor. While attending the sixth council of Baltimore, held in 1846, Bishop Hughes was summoned to Washington by Secretary of State Bu-

* Hassard's Life of Archbishop Hughes.

chanan, ostensibly to consult as to the appointment of
Catholic chaplains for the army, then engaged in the
Mexican War, but, it is said, in reality with a view to
sending the bishop as a special peace envoy to Mexico.
This was never known positively, as he did not go, and
would never speak of the matter afterward. In 1847
he received an invitation from John Quincy Adams,
John C. Calhoun, and other distinguished statesmen, to
preach before Congress in the Capitol at Washington.
He chose for his text, " Christianity the Only Source
of Moral, Social, and Political Regeneration."

In the fall of 1850 New York was elected into an
archiepiscopal see, with Boston, Hartford, Albany, and
Buffalo as suffragan sees. In 1854 he, with other
American prelates, accepted the invitation of Pope Pius
IX. to attend the assembly of bishops from the whole
Catholic world, gathered to take part in the ceremonies attendant on the definition of the dogma of the Immaculate Conception. On his return to New York he
commenced the erection of a church, the ninety-ninth
built and consecrated under his personal supervision,
in honor of the Immaculate Conception. This church
was consecrated May 15, 1858. Three months later
the corner-stone of the new cathedral of St. Patrick, at
Fifth Avenue and Fiftieth Street, was laid, in the presence of over one hundred thousand people. In 1859
he was very outspoken in his sympathy for Pope Pius
IX. He issued a vigorous pastoral on the subject of
the pontiff's troubles, which was so gratefully received
by his Holiness that he ordered it printed at the Propaganda in both Italian and English, a distinction never before conferred on a pastoral at Rome. He also collected
$53,000 in aid of the Holy Father's depleted treasury.

At the beginning of the late Civil War Archbishop Hughes was often consulted by President Lincoln and Secretary Seward, and in 1861 he was chosen for a special mission to Europe. His mission is briefly outlined in a letter which he wrote about that time, in which he says he went as the friend of both North and South alike. He went away with *carte-blanche*, to do and say anything that he should think proper for the interests of the country.

The last institution established by him was Saint Joseph's Theological Seminary, at Troy. It was moved from Fordham, and the buildings and ground sold to the Jesuit Fathers. His last sermon was delivered in June, 1863, at the dedication of a church, and his last public address was made from his balcony, the following month, during the draft riots. This address was delivered at the request of Governor Seymour, who asked him to do so in the hope that the archbishop's influence might tend to quell the excitement then raging in the city. He was obliged to remain seated on account of his feeble health.

His work was done. The task assigned to him had been faithfully performed. There remained nothing for him to do but to pass quietly away to the reward he had so well earned. His death was peaceful and happy. On Wednesday preceding he had received the last sacraments from his confessor, the Reverend William Quinn. From Friday (New-Year's day, 1864) until his death he had frequent spasms, followed by intervals of unconsciousness. About seven o'clock, Sunday evening, he had one of these attacks. "When it was over, he laid his head back on the pillow, closed his eyes, breathed quickly and gently for a few minutes,

and died with a smile about his lips, while Bishop
McCloskey was reciting the prayers of the Church for
a departing soul." *

On Tuesday the body was removed to the cathedral,
where, clad in episcopal robes, with mitre and crosier,
it lay for two days, on the very spot where, twenty-six
years before, he had knelt for consecration. It was es-
timated that no fewer than two hundred thousand persons viewed the remains.

On Thursday, January 7th, the anniversary of his
consecration, the funeral was held, and the remains deposited in one of the vaults under the altar of the
cathedral. Mr. Hassard says of this ceremony: " It
was perhaps the most imposing ceremony of the kind
ever witnessed in New York. Eight bishops and
nearly two hundred priests took part in the services.
The funeral discourse was pronounced by Bishop Mc-
Closkey, and mass was celebrated by Bishop Timon.
The body was deposited in a vault under the cathedral, by the side of the previous bishops of New York.
The courts and other public offices were closed on the
day of the funeral, and resolutions of sorrow and con-
dolence were passed by the State Legislature and the
Common Council."

* Hassard's Life of Archbishop Hughes.

CHAPTER IV.

THE FOUNDING OF THE COLLEGE TO THE ADVENT OF THE JESUITS.

WE have already noted in a former chapter that the one dominant thought of Archbishop Hughes's life, the thought that was ever uppermost in his mind, that seemed to influence his every action, was his solicitude in the cause of Catholic education. For two years he carried on an unequal struggle against the proselytizing system of education then followed in the common schools, a system as unconstitutional and as much opposed to the spirit of a republican government as it was dangerous to the preservation of the Catholic faith. But, though deeply interested in that all-important fight, he found time to turn his attention to the needs of higher education, and when his efforts for the improvement of the common schools were finally crowned with victory, he devoted all his energy toward supplying that other scarcely less pressing need.

We have seen how Bishop Dubois attempted the establishment of a college at Nyack, and how the buildings were destroyed by fire almost on the eve of their completion ; and we have also alluded to that good prelate's transfer of the field of his enterprise to Brooklyn, and his subsequent abandonment of the entire scheme. Such, then, was the state of affairs when Bishop Hughes

4

arrived in New York, and as soon as the disposal of more urgent matters left him comparatively free, he set about the task of completing the work begun by Bishop Dubois. The seminary at Lafargeville was the first fruit of his labors in this direction. But a very short trial convinced him of the utter futility of an effort to maintain an institution, especially a school for secular training, in a place so far removed from the metropolis, and he looked around in the neighborhood of New York for a suitable site on which to erect an-other college.

Fordham, at that time a village of Westchester County, among other places was brought to the bish-op's notice in' the course of his search. The Rose Hill estate, with its beautiful situation, its spacious grounds, and its historic interest, at once attracted him. At that time the village of Fordham was situated at a point farther west than its present location, the rail-road had not yet been constructed, and in the neigh-borhood of Rose Hill there were but a few isolated farm - houses, while the rows of ill - kept, unsightly buildings which, until a short time ago, disfigured the approach to the college grounds, did not make their ap-pearance until many years later. The bishop imme-diately entered into negotiations which resulted in the purchase of the property by him through Mr. Andrew Carrigan. Bishop Dubois, who was rapidly failing in both mind and body, was unable to take part in the negotiations. One result of his mental weakness was that he was extremely tenacious of his dignity, and keenly sensitive of anything like a slight. One of the clergymen of the diocese, to whom the bishop was par-ticularly attached, undertook the task of telling him of

the intended purchase by his coadjutor, and added in a
conciliatory tone : "You see, bishop, it was better that
he should appear in the matter, and not you ; he has
just come here and is not known yet." "Ah !" replied
the old bishop, "but they soon will know him." *

But the most difficult part of the task yet remained
to be done. The cost of the estate was $30,000, and
$10,000 was required to fit the buildings then on the
premises for the reception of students. To meet this
expense the bishop had not a dollar, but he was fertile
in expedients, and was not a long time in devising means
to raise the necessary funds. Nothing daunted at the
task that confronted him, he set to work soliciting subscriptions from wealthy Catholics throughout the diocese. He then went abroad and collected large sums
of money in Europe. The fund was completed by
small loans, for which interest was charged at the rate
of five per cent.

June 24, 1841, fifty years ago, the new college was
formally opened and started on its career under the
patronage of St. John the Baptist. No account of the
ceremonies of that opening day has come down to us,
and the papers at the time are all strangely silent on
the subject. However, the ceremonies took place, and
the following September the students of the new college assembled to begin the first scholastic year. It
was a triumph for Bishop Hughes, and, could he have
foreseen on that day the future that was in store for
his modest school, what would have been his emotions ?

The faculty of St. John's during its first year comprised some notable men. The first president was his

* Bishop Bayley's Discourse on the Life and Character of the Most Reverend Archbishop Hughes.

Eminence the late Cardinal McCloskey, then simply Dr. McCloskey, who hàd been taken from his pastoral duties at St. Joseph's Church, New York, to fill the presidential chair of the new college. Dr. McCloskey was a man highly esteemed for his talents and ability, and in every way fitted for his new position. In addition to performing the duties of president, he acted as professor of rhetoric and belles-lettres. The Reverend Ambrose Manahan, a distinguished divine, and author of a work entitled "Triumphs of Catholicity," was vice-president and professor of Greek and mathematics; the chair of moral philosophy and Hebrew was filled by the Reverend Felix Vilanis, D.D., and the Reverend John J. Conroy, afterward Bishop of Albany, was professor of Latin. The Reverend Edward O'Neill, who also acted in the capacity of treasurer, was professor of physics and chemistry. Mr. John Harley, who succeeded Dr. McCloskey in the presidency, and was subsequently secretary to Bishop Hughes, was prefect of discipline and instructor in book-keeping, and the Reverend Bernard Llaneza, Mr. Oertel, and Mr. McDonald were instructors in Spanish, German, and French, respectively. In addition to these there were six lay tutors whose names do not appear on the records.

Even at that early date, at that early stage of development of Fordham, she numbered among her professors and students many men who have since become famous. Among the former, besides Cardinal McCloskey, Bishop Conroy, and Father Manahan, were the Reverend J. Roosevelt Bayley, who was president for a year immediately preceding the advent of the Jesuits, and who afterward succeeded to the Archbishopric of Baltimore; the Reverend Bernard McQuaid,

CARDINAL McCLOSKEY,

1ST PRESIDENT.

who is now Bishop of Rochester; the Reverend Mr.
McFarland, afterward Bishop of Hartford, and the
Honorable John B. Stallo, who was professor of chem-
istry and physics previous to, and during the first
year of, the Jesuit *régime*. Mr. Stallo was afterward
raised to a place on the bench in Ohio, and during
President Cleveland's administration was appointed
United States Minister to Rome.

It may not be out of place here to devote a little
space to a review of the life of Dr. McCloskey, the
first president of St. John's, and destined to be the
first American Cardinal. He was born in Brooklyn,
in 1810. At that time there were but three Catholic
churches in New York and none in Brooklyn, and the
faithful in the latter, then isolated, locality were obliged to cross the river in small boats and bear in-
numerable hardships in order to hear mass and perform the other duties of their religion. It was not
until 1823 that a Catholic church, the first ever built
in Brooklyn, was erected at the corner of Jay and
Chapel Streets.

Determining to study for the priesthood, young
McCloskey, after passing through one of the parochial
schools in New York, was sent to Mount St. Mary's,
Emmettsburg, the "nursery of the Catholic Church in
America," and after a brilliant career in the college
course, from which he graduated with high honors, he
commenced his studies for the priesthood. On January 9, 1834, at the age of twenty-five, he was ordained
by Bishop Dubois in St. Patrick's Cathedral, Mott
Street, New York, and was granted the privilege of
continuing his studies for two years at the College of
the Propaganda, Rome.

Five years after his return he was appointed to the presidency of St. John's College and St. Joseph's Seminary at Fordham, which positions he held until 1843, when, the college being firmly established, he was called away to other fields where there was greater need for his peculiar talents. March 16, 1844, ten years and one month after his elevation to the priesthood, he was consecrated Bishop of Axiere, *in partibus infidelium,* and coadjutor to Bishop Hughes. In 1847 he was appointed first bishop of the new diocese of Albany, where he remained seventeen years. During that time he built St. Mary's Cathedral and established branch houses of many religious orders. He left Albany to return to New York as coadjutor again to Archbishop Hughes, and on the death of the latter prelate became Archbishop of New York.

March 15, 1875, the news was cabled from Rome that Archbishop McCloskey had been honored as no American had ever been honored before, by being raised to the dignity of the cardinalate. Six weeks later, on the altar at which he was ordained priest and consecrated bishop, the ceremony of investing him with the insignia of his new office was performed, the red hat being placed on his head by Archbishop Bayley, of Baltimore. He continued in the active management of the diocese until 1880, when his failing health necessitated the appointment of a coadjutor. The present archbishop, then Bishop Corrigan, of Newark, was chosen for the trying position, and, on the death of the cardinal, succeeded him. At 12.50 A.M. Saturday, October 10th, the cardinal passed quietly away, having received all the sacraments of the church. He was buried under the main altar of the cathedral. He

ARCHBISHOP BAYLEY,

3D PRESIDENT.

showed to the last the same gentle, loving spirit which distinguished him through life. He was beloved and revered by his own flock, and honored and respected by people of every shade of religious belief. The New York *Sun*, in an editorial on the dead cardinal, said : " His learning, his piety, his humility, his truly Christian zeal, earned for him the universal respect which will be to-day manifested as his body is carried to the tomb.

" The first American cardinal has died at a time when all Christians are ready to honor his memory as that of a man who has done measureless service in the cause of religion, good morals, and humanity. . . . Protestants and Catholics will join in sincerely mourning the first American cardinal as a Christian hero lost. *Requiescat in pace.*"

Returning, we will again take up the thread of the narrative. In the fall of 1841 the little bark, so happily launched less than three months before, began its eventful voyage. September of that year saw the opening of the first school term, the doors of Rose Hill College, as it was known at that time, were thrown open, and the work of instruction begun. There were about fifty students in the house at the time, many of whom are now living. The Reverend P. F. Dealy, S.J., who was president of the college from 1882 to 1885, and for many years previous a zealous worker at St. Francis Xavier's College, New York, and spiritual director of the Xavier Union (now the Catholic Club) was among those who saw the infant institution take its first faltering steps. After the arrival of the Jesuits he entered their novitiate, and has since become one of the most distinguished members of the order.

Mr. Paul Thébaud, of Mount Vernon, now a prominent merchant in New York, and his brother Gustav, a leading lawyer, also of New York; the Reverend James Hughes, A.M., LL.D., and Vicar-General of the Diocese of Hartford; Father Merrick, S.J., President of St. Francis Xavier College, New York; Mr. Lawrence O'Connor, '48, a well-known architect of New York; the Reverend Patrick McGovern, A.M., '48, of New York; Judge Dodge, '49, of Perrysburg, O.; Mr. Paul Berger, '46, and Mr. John F. Gray, '48, of New York; Mr. William Burke, '46, of Harrisburg, Pa., and Mr. James Reynolds, of Corona, L. I., are also among the few living now who remember the first years of Fordham College. About this time came Sylvester H. Rosecrans, afterward Bishop of Columbus, and a brother of General William H. Rosecrans of the United States Army; and Vicar-General William Keegan, of the diocese of Brooklyn. But these are both dead, as, indeed, are most of those who attended the college at the time.

We have elsewhere described the buildings as they stood at the time of their purchase by Bishop Hughes. In place of the brick wings of the main building as they now stand, were two one-story extensions, also of brick, the one on the south having been used by Mr. Moat as a conservatory. The ground at the rear of this building, which is now the campus, was rough and hilly, and useless as a playground. In the centre of the present First Division field was a hill, on the farther side of which was the quarry from which the stone was taken in 1845 to build the seminary and church.*

* The stone used in building Senior Hall was quarried in the rock overlooking the Bronx, and that used in Science Hall in the rock near the same quarry, in what is now part of the Bronx Park.

The students in the theological seminary were lodged and taught in the college buildings. The present sodality chapel, on the second floor of the main building, served as the seminarians' study, hall, and class-room. On this floor was also the library. " It was here," says Father Dealy, " I made my first speech in 1843, on the occasion of a reception given by Bishop Hughes to several bishops and other prelates."

About this time the "castle," joined to the south wing, the corresponding building on the north, and the old Second Division building, which was torn down in 1890, were erected. A wooden shed connected the Second Division building with the main building.

In 1843 Dr. McCloskey was taken from Fordham, and the Reverend John B. Harley, who had been a member of the faculty since the college was opened, was appointed to succeed him. The college had made wonderful progress in these two years. The number of students had been doubled, the grounds improved, new buildings erected, and the standard of studies considerably advanced. Father Harley's ill-health, however, did not permit him to enjoy the honor of presiding over this growing institution for any great length of time, and the following year he resigned and accompanied Bishop Hughes to Europe in the capacity of secretary. He was succeeded as president of St. John's by Father Bayley, afterward Archbishop of Baltimore.

Under Father Bayley Fordham College flourished and advanced as it had done under his predecessors. Every year saw some improvement. The seminary and chapel, to the northwest of the college buildings, were soon begun, and in 1845 were ready for occupation. They are both handsome buildings and add considerably to the beauty of the property. The interior of the seminary has been much altered since its dedication to the instruction of the small boy, but outwardly it is the same to-day as when first built, except perhaps for the mass of creeping vines which covers its entire front, and which, together with its latticed windows and peculiar style of architecture, lends to the building a charming air of antiquity. The spire that originally surmounted the bell-tower on the chapel was long ago removed, as it had begun to decay, but otherwise it has suffered no outward change.

About this time (1845), Bishop Hughes was contemplating a change in the management of the college. He had during his administration introduced a great many religious orders into the diocese, and he wished to place Rose Hill College entirely in the hands of some regular order, devoted to educational work. With this end in view, he made overtures to the Jesuits who had charge of St. Mary's College, Ky., and the result of the negotiations was an agreement by which they were to come to New York, and take possession of Rose Hill. He did not call upon the Jesuits of the Maryland province, because he feared they would make Fordham secondary to Georgetown, and keep it so, whereas he wished it to become in time the first Catholic college in the country, a position to which its proximity to the great commercial centre of the country would seem to entitle it.

In the meantime the course of study at the college, under the successful management of Dr. McCloskey, and Fathers Harley and Bayley, had advanced at such a pace, and attained so high a standard, that it was decided to apply for articles of incorporation. This was done, and April 10, 1846, the act of incorporation was passed, raising St. John's College, Fordham, to the rank of a university, with the power to grant degrees in theology, law, medicine, and arts. The incorporators were Jacob Harvey, Peter A. Hargous, John McKeon, James R. Bayley, John Harley, John McCloskey, William Starrs, Hugh Kelly, and David Bacon, afterward Bishop of Portland. The same month, Fathers William Stack Murphy and Augustus Thébaud, of the Society of Jesus, arrived from St. Mary's and were incorporated into the faculty. The following summer the whole community arrived, the institution passed into their hands, and the opening of the Fall term found the new university under an entirely new management; for although the seminary was not included in the purchase of Rose Hill, it was placed under the care of the Jesuits, and its classes were taught by Jesuit professors.

CHAPTER V.

HAVING thus far reviewed the train of events that led gradually up to the transfer of Fordham College to the Jesuit fathers, we will now turn aside from the direct course of my narrative to give a brief account of the previous history of those learned men. They came direct from St. Mary's College, at Mount Mary, Ky., where they had been for fifteen years. St. Mary's, therefore, was the immediate ancestor of Fordham, as Fordham is the mother-house of all the Jesuit houses in the States of New York and New Jersey. They came originally from France, by way of New Orleans, at the request of Bishop Flaget, of Bardstown, Ky., and took charge of St. Mary's under very peculiar circumstances. In 1829, the bishop had written to the Jesuit authorities in France, offering to turn St. Joseph's College, at Bardstown, over to their care. By some accident their letter, accepting the offer, miscarried, and the bishop judging by their apparent silence that his offer was not favorably received, made other and permanent arrangements for St. Joseph's.

The acceptance of the bishop's offer having been despatched, Fathers Peter Chazelle, Nicholas Petit, and Peter Labadiere, with Brother Corne, all of the Society of Jesus, set sail on November 19, 1830, from Pauillac, near Bordeaux, France, for New Or-

leans, La. They anchored at the island of Gua-
daloupe, where Father Chazelle preached, on January 5, 1831, and fifteen days later they arrived at
their destination. Here, at the invitation of Bishop
De Neckere, they remained about two months, and in
the meantime Father Chazelle, who was superior of
the little colony, wrote to Bishop Flaget, announcing
their arrival in compliance with his invitation, and their
readiness to accept the charge intended for them. This
threw the bishop into a quandary, as he had already
disposed of St. Joseph's; but, nevertheless, he extended
a hearty welcome to the Jesuits, and requested them to
come on to Bardstown. Accordingly, Fathers Chazelle
and Petit started northward, leaving Father Labadiere
and Brother Corne to establish a house in New Orleans.

Arrived at Bardstown, the two Jesuits assisted in the
college and seminary until the following July, when,
as there was no prospect of a solution of the difficulty,
they joined with the bishop in a novena to St. Ignatius,
that they might find through his intercession a way
out of their awkward position. Their prayers were
not unheard, for before the novena was finished the
bishop received a letter from the Reverend William
Byrne, president of St. Mary's College, asking that he
be allowed to turn his institution over to the Jesuits.

St. Mary's College and Seminary was situated on a
productive farm, then in Washington County, but now
in Marion County, Ky., which had been purchased
in 1820 from Mr. Joseph Ray, by the saintly missionary, Father Charles Nerinckx. It was his intention to establish here an industrial school for the education of boys in the useful trades, with a course of

studies for higher education, should any of his pupils
desire it. Sailing for Belgium in 1820, he left the
church of St. Charles and Mount Mary, as he called the
newly purchased farm, in charge of Father Byrne.
During his absence the latter conceived the idea of es-
tablishing a seminary at Mount Mary, and fitted up an
abandoned still-house which stood on the property, for
that purpose, and when Father Nerinckx returned from
Europe he found his original plans completely upset
and the new seminary in a flourishing condition, having
all the students its limited quarters could accommodate.
In spite of several unfortunate accidents (for St. Mary's
was three times consumed by fire before the advent of
the Jesuits) and limited means the seminary pros-
pered. Father Byrne was unable to procure a sufficient number of competent teachers, and he began to
employ the older and more trustworthy of his pupils
for that purpose, a custom which was perpetuated by
the Jesuits.

But Father Byrne was not eminently fitted to direct
a large educational institution, and he himself was
among the first to realize that fact. So, when the news
reached him of the arrival of the Jesuits and the unfortunate misunderstanding about St. Joseph's, he resolved to resign the presidency of St. Mary's and ten-
der that institution to the newly arrived fathers. He,
therefore, wrote to the bishop, as above stated, making
the offer and asking simply to be allowed to keep his
saddle-horse and ten dollars in money. This offer settled the difficulty at once, and the problem which had
for so long disturbed good Bishop Flaget's mind was
solved at last.

In the summer of 1831 Fathers Chazelle and Petit

entered on their new charge. But here a fresh barrier presented itself, which they had to overcome before they could take entire charge of the college. This was their insufficient knowledge of the English language, and the character and customs of American boys. But Father Byrne disposed of this obstacle by offering to remain and act as president, until such time as the strangers should have overcome this difficulty. This he did and retained the office until June of 1833, when he died from an attack of Asiatic cholera which was prevalent at the time. A few days later Father Maguire, S.J., who had come from France in the spring of 1832, with Fathers Gilles and Legouais, to join the little community, died of the same disease. His body was afterward taken to Fordham, and now lies in the little college cemetery at that place.

St. Mary's was now entirely under the direction of the Jesuits, and Father Chazelle was president. Both he and Father Petit had made such progress in learning English that they were able to preach from time to time in the parish church of St. Charles, and Father Chazelle was even emboldened to enter into a wider field of literary work. He wrote several dramas, one of which was produced by the students every year from 1834 until 1846, when the community moved to Fordham. These plays, which accompanied the annual exhibition, were, according to a fancy of Father Chazelle, enacted in the woods, and to this we may trace the custom, which is still religiously observed at Fordham, of holding the Commencement exercises in the open air, under a tent spread on the lawn for that purpose. The practice has many advantages, not the least of which is the comfort of the audience, who, at that season of the year must feel much more at ease in an open tent than in the close confinement of a hall.

In 1835 Fathers Evremond and Fouché, who had entered the novitiate in the fall of 1831, were added to the community. Father Fouché was director of the seminary at St. Mary's when the first two Jesuits arrived there. He died in Fordham in 1870, and was buried in the college cemetery. In 1836 came from France Father William Stack Murphy, whom we have mentioned, and Father Nicholas Point, who afterward became famous as a missionary in the Rocky Mountains. Father Point is still living at St. Mary's College, at Montreal, over ninety years of age. Father Murphy at once became a great favorite among the students. He was famous as a literary man, and attracted general attention by his perfect elocution, the purity of his English, and his happy conversational powers. In 1837 he succeeded Father Chazelle as superior of the community and president of the college, for both of which positions he was eminently fitted.

In 1837 the fathers made application to the Kentucky Legislature for a charter of incorporation, to give them all the powers of a university. To bring this about and urge the matter in the legislative halls, Father Murphy and Father Robert Abell, the latter an American Jesuit and a famous orator, went to Frankfort. Father Abell was invited to address the Senate on the subject, and those who listened to him that day, men who had listened to the most eloquent speakers of an era that abounded in finished orators, declared that his speech excelled any they had ever heard. The application was favorably received, the desired charter promptly granted, and on January 21,

1837, St. Mary's took its place among the universities
of the State. The first meeting of trustees was held
February 2, 1837, and the first annual Commencement,
at which diplomas were awarded, was held in the summer of 1838.

The subsequent progress of St. Mary's soon placed it
in the front rank of the colleges of the State. Many
men who have since become famous, were connected
with St. Mary's during those later years of the Jesuit
management. Father Chazelle went to Canada in 1839,
and was mainly instrumental in having the Jesuits introduced into British America. Father Petit was employed chiefly on missionary work, and Father Evremond established a house in Louisville, to which was
afterward attached a successful day-school under the
direction of Father John Larkin. Father Larkin was
in later years president of Fordham, and his memory
is still fondly cherished in the heart of every old Fordham student who had the good fortune to know him.

In 1837 Father Legouais established the Parthenian
Sodality, which was afterward transferred to Fordham
and is now the oldest constituted society among the
students of that institution. He introduced the custom
of daily mass for the sodalists, until then unheard of,
preceded by ten minutes' meditation. Father Legouais
is described as a man of diminutive stature, with un-
usually short legs, and in those days of rough roads,
when everybody was obliged to travel on horseback,
many amusing mishaps befell him. If he once dis-
mounted he could not regain his place in the saddle
again until some chance passer-by appeared to assist
him.* Father Driscoll, who was afterward promi-

* A story is told to the effect that a Protestant gentleman, who had entered

5

nently connected with St. John's, and was rector of St.
Francis Xavier's College for several years, was among
the first members of the sodality.   He had a very interesting history.   Before he entered the Jesuit novitiate he was a stone-mason, and by his superior intelli-
gence attracted the attention of Father De Luynes,
pastor of the cathedral at Bardstown, who, feeling
that the young man was called to higher things, sent
him to St. Mary's.   In 1838 he entered the novitiate
under Father Gilles, who had just been appointed
Master of Novices, and was joined a year later by
Father Larkin, from Montreal, Canada, and.in 1841 by
his patron, Father De Luynes. ⌐Father Driscoll lived
to a ripe old age.   He, with Father De Luynes and
Father Larkin, sleeps peacefully in the little cemetery
at Fordham.

In 1839 the Reverend Augustus Thébaud, afterward
the fourth president, and first Jesuit president of St.
John's, arrived from France with several lay-brothers,
and about the same time the Reverend F. William
Gockeln, who also succeeded subsequently to the presidential chair of Fordham, and who is described as "a
tall, handsome young Prussian" arrived from Canada,
attracted thither by Father Larkin.   Among the other
fathers who were since well known at St. John's were
Fathers Lebreton, Du Merle, and Maréchal.   The first
two lie in the Fordham cemetery.

his boy at St. Mary's, hurried to the president a few minutes later, and stipu-
lated that under no circumstances should his boy be allowed to say mass.   In
explanation of his extraordinary condition, he said that he had just seen one
of the small boys in the chapel in the act of celebrating mass.   Father Chazelle, the president, immediately repaired to the chapel, accompanied by the
anxious father, and there found Father Legouais officiating at the altar.   The
stranger seeing him from the rear had taken him for a small boy.

The college was then progressing rapidly. In the classics, physical sciences, and mathematics it especially excelled. Father Legouais attempted to establish a class of Philosophy in Latin, with Bouvier as a text-book, but it was a failure. Father Larkin afterward began instruction in logic, in English, and Father De Luynes lectured in English on general and special metaphysics, both of which ventures were successful. Rhetoric, belles-lettres, mathematics, modern languages, and music were not neglected, and the college took another step forward. Father Thébaud was an enthusiastic Greek scholar, and his courses in higher mathematics, chemistry, and physics were eminently successful. He wrote a learned and scholarly paper, in French, on the Mammoth Cave, which was rendered into elegant English by Father Murphy.

About 1845 the Jesuits began to experience some trouble. Exactly what the difficulty was is not generally known, but it is supposed that it was caused by some difference with Bishop Chabrat, coadjutor to Bishop Flaget. Old Bishop Flaget was most favorable to the Jesuits, and is known to have said on one occasion since their departure from his diocese: "I have grieved without ceasing ever since the fathers left my diocese two years ago." But the trouble had arisen, and there was no way to avoid it. The Louisville house was abandoned in March, 1846, the fathers returning to St. Mary's. About this time the arrangement with Bishop Hughes was perfected, by which the college at Fordham was sold to the fathers of St. Mary's, and Fathers Murphy and Thébaud left on April 19, 1846, arriving at Fordham on April 28th. They were kindly received by the professors at that place, and at once incorporated into the faculty. Father Larkin took his departure on July 2d, arriving at St. John's on the 18th.

When it became definitely known that the Jesuits were leaving St. Mary's general sorrow and excitement prevailed, and the indignation against Bishop Chabrat, who was considered responsible for their departure, was openly expressed. He went to France the following year, and resigned. His action was ascribed by the people of the diocese to the outcry against him.

The work of packing up the movable property, the books, scientific apparatus, and specimens of natural history, was vigorously prosecuted, and by the beginning of August, 1846, the last of it had been despatched on its way to New York. The fathers, scholastics, and brothers left Kentucky in four bands, between July 21st and 31st, and arrived at Fordham between August 2d and 11th. Among them were Fathers Driscoll, Nash (now at Troy, N. Y.), De Luynes, Henry Hudon (now at Montreal), and Gockeln, and Brothers Hennen, Crowe, and Ledoré. The last to leave the old place, and perhaps the most pained at the parting, were Fathers Fouché and Legouais, who did not go until August 10th. The only survivors of those who left Kentucky for Fordham are Fathers Nash and Hudon. St. John's, as already stated, had been incorporated in the spring of 1846, and in September the Jesuits started in anew, in a strange place and among a strange people.

CHAPTER VI.

WE have already outlined, with as much attention
to detail as our space would allow, the successive
stages through which St. John's had passed, from the
inception of the idea to the sale of the school to the
Jesuits. That under their management it would rise
to opulence and power was, to Archbishop Hughes's
mind, almost a foregone conclusion. He had the example of St. Mary's to help him in reaching this conclusion, and the sequel has proven the soundness of his
judgment. The work so auspiciously begun by Dr.
McCloskey, and followed up so well by his two successors, was enthusiastically taken up by the new
management. That it has been vigorously and judi-
ciously prosecuted since that time, there need be no
doubt. We have only to look at the St. John's of to-
day and compare it with the St. John's of that earlier
day, to find objective evidence to convince us. That
the college had progressed during its first few years of
existence to such an extent as to satisfy the expecta-
tions of its illustrious founder, is amply attested by
him in a pastoral letter of 1847, in which he says:

". . . In five short years St. John's College rose from the
condition of an unfinished house in a field to the cluster of buildings of which it is now composed ; and from an obscure Catholic

school, beginning with six students, to the rank and privileges of a
university. . . . We deem it an evidence of Almighty God's
approval that a numerous, learned, and pious community of the illustrious Society of Jesus—a society especially instituted for the
imparting of a high order of Christian education to youth—should
have been found willing to take charge of it permanently."

Could Archbishop Hughes return to earth on this fiftieth anniversary of Fordham College and see the result of his zeal and energy, the proportions to which his
little school had grown, he would not recognize it.
The college of 1846 and 1847, that stirred the good old
bishop's heart with pride, splendid as it certainly was,
was as nothing compared to the magnificent institution
that celebrates its golden jubilee this year.

To the reader familiar with the Fordham of to-day
the following description of the entrance to the college
grounds, from the pen of Father Nash, S.J., which appeared in a recent issue of the *Fordham Monthly*, will
certainly prove interesting :

" Stepping out of the car we glanced about for the
city, town, or village of Fordham. On the east side
there was no sign of it. Splendid shady trees occupied
the ground to the edge of the track. To the west were
a few scattered houses climbing up the hill which arose
gradually from the railroad. Our eyes failed to see
anything which we could call St. John's College. To
our inquiries came the answer that in Fordham there
are two boarding-schools for young gentlemen, both of
which are managed by ministers of the Gospel. This
information gave us very little light in our search. The
entrances to both were pointed out to us. A large,
heavy gate, which opened on to an avenue running directly east, and shaded by magnificent trees decked in

their August foliage, was the entrance to the college whose president was the Reverend Dr. Powell, an Episcopalian minister. Almost adjoining this, and at right angles with it, was a smaller gate, from which ran northward a foot-path flanked on the east side by a massive wall of stones without mortar, along which grew a row of 'ox-heart' cherry-trees. On the west side was, without any protecting barrier, a steep and threatening ravine. This we were informed was the entrance to the second college, thought to belong to Catholic priests. Passing through the small gate which opened into the 'narrow way,' we found ourselves on the property of St. John's College. A few moments' walk brought us to a point where the massive wall and row of cherry-trees turned eastward at right angles, and gave us a view of the solid building called Rose Hill College and the superb lawn sweeping in front of the buildings, something in the form of a semicircle, and gracefully descending to the railroad, which would be the diameter of the circle. Ascending the avenue into which our narrow path had suddenly been transformed at the abrupt term of the stone wall, we were amazed at the beauty of the scene spread out before us and around us. The grand appearance of the lawn, the site of the scattered buildings composing the college, the view of the railroad winding along the foot of the lawn, the hills rising west of the railroad as if straining to obtain one more glance at the sun disappearing beyond the royal Hudson, the picturesque location of the future Fordham, the compact and solid expression of old 'Rose Hill' residence now and for evermore 'St. John's College,' were surely capable of producing on the least sensitive nature an indelible impression."

And this was Fordham forty-five years ago! A glance at the Fordham of to-day will show the disparity. But let us follow the changes step by step, and feel our way gradually from the "unfinished house in a field" to Fordham College fifty years old.

Father Thébaud was the first Jesuit to assume the reins of government in the new school, and he handled them skilfully and well. He was, as we have already said, a man of almost exhaustive erudition, and the author of several well-known and widely read volumes. "The Irish Race," "Gentilism," and "The Church and the Gentile World," are among the best known of his works. "A perfect child in simplicity," said the late Vicar-General Keegan, of Brooklyn, "but a giant in everything sublime and useful, Father Thébaud was a man who would have been an ornament to any profession."

Father Thébaud had an able and efficient corps of professors to aid him in the management of the college. Father John Larkin was vice-president, prefect of studies, and professor of philosophy; Father Murphy was professor of rhetoric; Father Du Merle, first prefect of discipline; Father Lebreton as minister, and Mr. Stallo as professor of chemistry and physics. Father Thébaud's first care was to regulate the course of study. It was decided in January, 1847, that to obtain the degree of Bachelor of Arts, it was necessary that the aspirant be able to read with ease the works of Cicero or Livy, Virgil or Horace, Demosthenes or Homer, and to stand examination in arithmetic, algebra, geometry, and trigonometry.

The system of instruction established in the college was followed for the first year. According to this system there was one professor for each branch of study, but it was soon found that too much time was lost by the students in going from one class to another at the adjournment of the lectures. The frequent changes of professors, with many lesser disadvantages accompanying it, was found equally unsatisfactory. At the end of the first year the entire system was abolished, and a catalogue of Georgetown College having been procured in the meantime, the plan laid down in the *ratio studiorum* of the Jesuits was adopted. It was settled that the course should consist of three grammar classes, in which the rudiments were taught, and the classes of Humanities, or Belles-lettres, Rhetoric, and Philosophy. It was not then settled how many years should be devoted to philosophy, nor was anything definitely arranged for the classes of mathematics.

This plan has been considerably altered since that time. The Classical course now consists of seven instead of six classes. The elements of Latin, Greek, English, and other necessary branches are taught as before in the three grammar classes. The class of Classics, or *suprema grammatica*, the first of the undergraduate classes, is the step by which the student, emerging from the rudimentary studies of the grammar department, reaches the higher branches taught in the classes of Humanities, Rhetoric, and Philosophy. The first year of philosophy, at the close of which the degree of Bachelor of Arts is conferred, comprises a course in logic, general and special metaphysics, and the general principles of ethics and of civil society. A post-graduate course of one year in which the study of ethics is further prosecuted, and at the end of which the degree of Master of Arts is conferred, has been added.

Another addition to the original plan is the Commercial course, consisting of five classes. Into this course the study of the classics does not enter at all, the time being wholly given up to English and the study of business forms. Connected with this course is the Scientific Department, including the classes in Surveying, Electrical Engineering, Photography, and Analytical Chemistry. The Surveying class, under the direction of the professor, surveys the ground in the neighborhood of the college. Apart from both these courses, and in no way affected by them, is the mathematical course. The grading of a student in the regular course does not, in the least, affect his standing in the class of mathematics, until he reaches his senior, or philosophy year, when his rating in the former branch becomes an important factor in deciding his right to a diploma. Music, drawing, painting, and the modern languages are special studies.

We have already described the buildings that stood on the grounds at the time of its purchase in 1841, and the additions made prior to 1846. The wing at the south of the main building, on the site of the present chapel wing, was used as a study hall; the present parlor was the chapel, and the parlor was in the present rector's office. The north wing was utilized as a refectory for the students, an office which its more substantial successor now fills. Some of the classes, such as Physics, Chemistry, and Higher Mathematics, were taught in the main building. The other class-rooms were in a one-story brick building which ran eastward from the end of the south wing and connected with the three-story building known to fame in after-years as "the castle." In the castle were the music-rooms, reading-room, and first prefect's office.

Father Thébaud removed the shed which connected the mansion with the Second Division building, to a point northeast of the buildings, where it was afterward on the dividing line between Second and Third Divisions. In its place he erected the three-story brick building now standing there, in which are the music-rooms, wardrobe, and library. The physics class-room was in the cellar of this building. In 1849 an extension was built to the Second Division building. This entire structure was torn down in the summer of 1890 on the completion of the new Junior Hall, while the castle had disappeared a month or more previous, to make room for the new faculty building. The present infirmary was, at this time, occupied by a few Sisters of Charity who had charge of the domestic arrangements, but in 1847 it became the Jesuit novitiate. The scholastic novices remained there until 1850, when they were removed to Montreal; the coadjutor novices remained until 1859. The new seminary was ready for occupation this year, and the little cottage near it was occupied by Mr. Rodrigue, a brother-in-law of Archbishop Hughes.

CHAPTER VII.

THE year in which the new system was inaugurated was a remarkable year for Fordham. It saw a notable array of learned men on the faculty of the college. Fathers Daubresse and Duranquet, whose names have been familiar to generations of New Yorkers, were among the professors then. Fathers Murphy, Ryan, Driscoll, and Pottgeisser, Mr. Doucet and Mr. Hudon, and Brother Macé, have all since become well known. Famous among the singers on the faculty were Fathers Verheyden and Schiansky, and Messrs. Doucet and Glackmeyer. Father Schiansky had a remarkable history. He had been in former years a leading tenor singer in an opera company in Vienna, but with his wife had experienced a change of heart, and, after making a retreat in Rome, they, with the permission of the authorities of the Church, separated, she to go into a convent, and he to enter the Jesuit novitiate. Father Du Merle, of whom we have already spoken, was prefect of discipline; Father Legouais, and Mr. Tissot, who afterward became president of the college, were among the notable men of that time.

Fathers Nash and Ouellet, who with Father Tissot became famous during the war as chaplains in the army; Fathers Driscoll, Regnier, and Hudon were also to be seen at Fordham in those days.

REV. AUGUSTUS THÉBAUD, S.J.

4TH PRESIDENT.

But the most prominent figure of that period, the man who stands pre-eminent among his fellows, is Father William Stack Murphy. Father Murphy, it is needless to say, was an Irishman, and came of a family that had already supplied some distinguished members of the Irish hierarchy. His uncle, Bishop Murphy, of Cork, was a savant, and there was hardly a book-stall in the United Kingdom that he had not searched for rare volumes to furnish the shelves of his library. Father Murphy, like so many Catholic Irishmen of that time (he was born in the last decade of the eighteenth century), was educated in France, where he entered the Jesuit novitiate. Never again did he set foot on his native land. When he passed it on his way to America, he had permission to land and visit his mother, but, like St. Francis Xavier, who declined a similar privilege when passing through Spain on his way to the Indies, he denied himself and watched the shores of his native land fade from his view, and with them his only opportunity of ever meeting her again on earth. But if, in a spirit of mortification, he denied himself in a manner such as few had ever adopted before, still he thought of his mother, and thought of her tenderly, for Father Merrick, president of St. Francis Xavier's College, and an old Fordham student, tells us that Father Murphy often told his boys that "there had been a time when he wore long curls, and his mother thought him as handsome a boy as any of their mothers thought them."

When he came to Fordham, although he was little more than fifty years of age, his hair was perfectly white, his form was thin and spare, and the deep, thoughtful expression of his intellectual face was height-

ened by a pair of glasses. He was not an orator, although what he said carried weight and conviction with
it. His forte was literature; he was a great purist,
and an enthusiastic admirer of the classics of the last
century. Of his teaching it has been said: "There
may have been a method in it, as there is said to be in
some people's madness, but it would puzzle anyone to
find it out." Certain it is, however, that unique as his
system may have been, and odd the means by which he
attained his end, the fact remains that the goal was
reached, the end attained. For though his pupils came
to his hands the rawest of raw material, he turned them
out so wonderfully developed that the most stupid and
indolent would be able to accomplish something in the
way of literary work.

When a debate or other similar literary exercise was
in preparation it was his custom (for such affairs were
usually under his direction) to call the orators in turn
to his room, there to read aloud their productions.
The student would probably find him shaving, and then,
with his face covered with lather, gesticulating with
the razor in his hand, he would correct mistakes, point
out shortcomings, and sometimes, when thoroughly
warmed up, would hold forth for a half-hour for the
edification of his single listener. He had an inex-
haustible fund of stories, and had a quaint manner
of attaching great interest to the most commonplace
remarks. His class was said to be a source of pleasure and entertainment even to the most indolent
and indifferent, such was the charm of his manner
and the delightful way he had of imparting information.

Father Murphy was a constant sufferer from dyspepsia, but, unlike many victims of that irritating disease, he caused no discomfort to those who surrounded him. He kept his sufferings to himself, was uniformly kind and genial, and lived to a ripe old age, a constant source of pleasure and enjoyment to all who were associated with him. His malady was eventually the cause of his leaving New York, where he had been superior of the mission for several years. From New York he went directly to St. Louis, Mo., where he became superior of the province. From there he went to New Orleans, where he was at the time of the late war. While there he made the acquaintance of General Banks, with whom he became so intimate that when the people of the city wanted any favor or concession, they knew no surer means of having it granted than by securing the intercession of the "Yankee priest." He ended his days at New Orleans, at an advanced age.

Among the students who figured in that first epoch in the history of Fordham, as a university, we find the names of many men who have since served church or state faithfully and well. First among them, for many reasons, from the dignity of the position which he afterward attained, from the character he sustained in college, and the esteem in which he was held by both faculty and students, was Bishop Rosecrans. He was among the first students to enter the new college, and immediately established a reputation for steadiness, uprightness, and studiousness that soon placed him in the front rank among his fellows, and enabled him to exert a wonderful influence over them. He was one of the four who received the degree of Bachelor of Arts at the second annual Commencement of the college, July 15, 1847.* His address on that occasion was pronounced a brilliant and scholarly effort, and was published in full in the report of the exercises which appeared the following day in the New York *Herald*. The three other young men to receive degrees on that memorable day were Peter McCarron, Thomas Dolan, both of whom, like Bishop Rosecrans, entered the priesthood, and, like him also, have gone over to the " great majority ; " and Andrew J. Smith, who is still delving in the " dusky purlieus of the law."

The published account of that commencement may possibly be of interest to our readers, so we reproduce it, in part, as it appeared in the *Herald* of July 16th :

The first annual Commencement of this newly incorporated college took place at Fordham yesterday afternoon. All the regular trains of cars on the Harlem Railroad were crowded during the morning, and at 1 o'clock P.M. an extra train of six cars was despatched to take up passengers, whose business or other engagements kept them in the city until that hour.

The exercises were conducted in a large tent, erected for the occasion on the beautiful lawn in front of the college buildings, where, after the passengers from the last train had taken their places, there were present about two thousand persons, among whom we observed members of the city legislature, officers of the army, and other public persons, besides hundreds of pretty girls, beautiful young ladies, and good-looking matrons.

On the stage were seated Bishop Hughes, Bishop McCloskey, Joseph R. Chandler, Esq., of Philadelphia, Rev. Mr. Starrs, Rev. Mr. Bayley, Rev. Mr. C. Loudon, Canada, and Rev. Messrs. McCarron, O'Neil, McLellan, of this city, and the faculty of the

---

* In the reports of this event which appeared in the daily papers at the time, it is called the first annual Commencement. This is wrong. The first Commencement was held in 1846, immediately after the charter was received. At this first Commencement Bishop Hughes, in the course of his address, announced that the college was to be given into the charge of the Jesuits.

college—Father Augustus J. Thébaud, President; Father John Larkin, Vice-President; Father William S. Murphy, Father Charles De Luynes, Father Louis Petit, Father H. Du Merle.

There were only four graduates, upon whom devolved the duty of delivering the orations, of which one was a discourse on Russia, by Mr. Charles De Bull.* It was a creditable performance, showing considerable historical knowledge and a happy turn of thought—reflection based upon past occurrences.

The next oration was a Latin performance, *De Laudibus Linguæ Lat. Oratio*, by P. McGovern, who articulated clearly, and acquitted himself in all respects well, in a Latin speech of considerable length.

The third was a discourse on O'Connell, by P. McCarron, who, with a modest introduction, prefaced some quite eloquent remarks in laudation of the lamented Irish statesman.

A discourse on "Chivalry," a good composition, was delivered by Mr. Andrew J. Smith, who was also the honored graduate who delivered the Valedictory Address.

The last discourse . . . was of course the best, and was in consequence reserved till the last. It was written and delivered by Mr. S. H. Rosecrans, whose father is now Professor of Civil Engineering at West Point. It was entitled "Nothing Original."

Here follows the address, which we omit.

Next came the ceremony of conferring degrees. The degree of Bachelor of Arts was conferred upon Messrs. Thomas Dolan, Andrew Smith, S. M. Rosecrans, and P. McCarron. Mr. Smith was also honored with the degree of Master of Arts. The diplomas were given to the young gentlemen. The vice-president, Father Larkin, made a very happy address to the graduates, reminding them of their prospective duties, etc. The premiums were then distributed to the students and scholars of the preparatory schools.

Then follows a long list of prize-winners in various branches.

---

* This is an error; neither Mr. De Bull nor Mr. McGovern were graduated that year.

6

The valedictory address was next delivered by Andrew J. Smith, A.B., who, in an able manner, took leave of his classmates and the faculty. Bishop Hughes, being requested, then came forward and made some very happy remarks, appropriate to the occasion, after which the assemblage broke up.

An interesting relic of this Commencement day came to light within the last few years and was given to the public through the columns of the *Fordham Monthly*. It is an address, written on paper once white, but which has become yellow and discolored at the hand of time. It reads as follows:

MR. ANDREW J. SMITH, MR. SYLVESTER ROSECRANS, MR. PETER McCARRON.

GENTLEMEN : I am commissioned by the faculty of St. John's College to hand to each of you a diploma of Bachelor of Arts. This diploma is the solemn and authentic proof of the favorable judgment which the Faculty of this institution, after due examination and mature consideration, have formed both of your intellectual capacity and of your moral conduct and principles. By these documents which are public, by the authority from which they emanate, by the object they have in view, and by the circumstances under which they are handed to you, we stand committed before the world, unless by the rectitude of your future conduct and steady application to your respective duties you justify our decision.

For, gentlemen, let me impress upon your minds that, by asking for and receiving the academic honors, you enter into a solemn and public engagement to show yourselves worthy of the distinction which is conferred on you. This distinction is conferred upon you, not in our name, but in the name and by the authority of the Republic, and to the Republic both we and you are responsible. If the Republic invests us with a discretionary power to decorate with these distinctions those whom we judge worthy, it expects, and it has a right to expect, that they should show themselves on all occasions, in word and in deed, friends of law and order, defenders of truth and justice, supporters of sound morality.

Receive your diploma of Bachelor of Arts, and remember the engagements which you contract.

A query accompanied the publication of this document, calling for information as to who delivered the address. It is more than probable that it was Father Larkin, because according to the newspaper report of the occurrence he addressed the graduates.

In the list of prize-winners to which I have alluded, the name that most frequently occurs is that of Charles De Bull. There is no record of his graduation, and he is not numbered among the alumni, yet he appears to have been among the foremost students of his time. Both his professors and fellow-students who have been known to express an opinion of him, have spoken of him in the highest terms. The late Father Doucet said : " De Bull was a boy the like of whom you will meet once in a lifetime. He had a wonderful influence for good among the other students," and Father Merrick speaks of him as "our St. Aloysius." He died in Rome.

Among the other students under Father Thébaud's presidency who have won distinction in the world and reflected credit on their *alma mater*, we may name Vicar-General William Keegan, of the diocese of Brooklyn, and Judge Henry H. Dodge, of Perrysburg, O., both of the class of '49. Vicar-General Keegan was a native of Ireland, although educated in this country, and was a warm personal friend in after-life of Father Thébaud. He died in May, 1890, at the age of sixty-six years. Judge Dodge, as I have said, was a classmate of Father Keegan, and since his graduation has followed the practice of law. It is said that in his school-days he was not very prepossessing, and was very awkward when he made his first speech. "But," says one who knew him then, "no one minded that; all we paid attention to was the precocious gravity and maturity of the young man."

There was Michael O'Connor, of Charleston, S. C., also of the class of '49, a fiery Secessionist and brother of Lawrence O'Connor who is mentioned in a previous chapter. He became a member of Congress after the war, and the degree of LL.D. was conferred on him by the college in 1881. The catalogue of that year records the awarding of the degree, and adds, in a footnote, that he "died since the degree was conferred." And we must not omit Father Merrick, to whom we have already referred more than once, "the irrepressible Merrick," as Judge Dodge has termed him. He was of the class of '50, entered the Society of Jesus, and is now president of St. Francis Xavier's College, New York. Other well-known students of that time were—the Very Reverend John A. Kelly, '51, Vicar-General of the diocese of Trenton, who died in February, 1891; Lawrence O'Connor and the Very Reverend James Hughes, Vicar-General of Hartford diocese, both of whom we mentioned before; the Reverend William Plowden Morrogh, '49, who became superior of St. Joseph's Ecclesiastical Seminary at Fordham, and afterward pastor of the Church of the Immaculate Conception, in New York; the Reverend Daniel Fisher, '48, first rector of Seton Hall College, South Orange, N. J.; Felix Kennedy, and Daniel Gray. The first to receive the degree of LL.D. from Fordham was the learned Dr. Orestes A. Brownson, on whom this distinguished honor was conferred in 1850.   Dr. John Gilmary Shea, the eminent Catholic historian, was a member of the faculty in 1848 and 1849.

Several changes worthy of note took place during the last years of Father Thébaud's presidency.   In 1850 the students' library was established, the room assigned for it being in the building where the music-rooms and wardrobe are now.   The previous year the annual retreat, which had hitherto been held during Lent, was given in October, which time has been selected ever since.

CHAPTER VIII.

FATHER THÉBAUD's successor in the presidency of
Fordham was the Reverend John Larkin, to whom we
have referred on more than one occasion in the preceding chapters of this work. He had entered the society in Kentucky, had come from that place to Fordham, and had been vice-president during the Jesuits'
first year there. He is described as one of the hand-
somest, most courtly, and most erudite men that Fordham had ever seen. He was a man among men, a man
once known never forgotten. "No man," says the late
Mr. Hassard, "who was at St. John's between 1851
and 1854 can speak of Father John Larkin without
a quickening pulse. For me, ever since I first saw
him, thirty-five years ago, the college has been filled
with his majestic presence." Mr. Hassard fairly idolized
Father Larkin, as indeed did nearly every student who
was connected with St. John's during those early years.

"A great many of the Jesuits," continues Mr. Hassard, "were fine-looking men, but none of us had ever
seen just such a type of masculine beauty as this, big
rosy Englishman. He was immensely stout. Soon
after he arrived, I remember taking a younger brother
of mine to a place where we could look at him across
the fence as he read his office in the garden. 'Isn't he
fat!' we exclaimed; and we both added: 'But how,

REV. JOHN LARKIN, S.J.

5TH PRESIDENT.

handsome he is! ' Although his face was too full, the
exquisite outlines of his classical features were not ob-
scured; he had the mouth of a young Greek god; in
his eye there was a singular union of mildness and
penetration; his large head was crowned with fine
silky brown hair, rather long and wavy, and brushed
well back from his broad forehead. His voice, like
that of most short-necked people of apoplectic habit,
was apt to be a little husky, but it was perfectly modu-
lated, and his enunciation was a marvel of distinctness.
To hear him talk was a lesson in elocution. Neither
his preaching nor his conversation gave you the idea
of labored precision; it was fluent, easy, direct, natural; but every word had its just emphasis and exact
pronunciation, and every sentence its sure balance.
There is a certain tone of speech rarely acquired except by persons of thorough education and high breed-
ing; it indicates familiarity with the best usages, refined taste, self-possession, composure. Father Larkin
had more of that than any man I ever met except
James Russell Lowell."

Such was Father Larkin as he appeared to an admiring pupil—genial, polished, scholarly, a perfect type of
the true Christian gentleman. His influence over the
students of Fordham was truly wonderful; and it was
an influence that did not cease to act when the student
went forth into the world free from the check and
restraint of college life, but it was carried forth and
remained in its effects long after many another impression had worn away.

A little incident happened during the first year of
Father Larkin's presidency that aptly illustrates the
unreasoning manner in which the average boy will act,

and the wrong motives which he will ascribe for acts which he does not understand. For some unknown reason no holiday was given on St. Patrick's day of Father Larkin's first year as president. The boys demanded a holiday, but their request was denied. It immediately became noised among the students that in thus refusing he was actuated by prejudice, and that being an Englishman, his antipathy to anything Irish had caused him to take his stand against the holiday. It was only required that a rumor of this kind be started for belief to seize a firm hold on the boys, and a plot for revenge was set on foot. On the evening of March 16th, when the boys assembled for prayers, everyone was well supplied with marbles of the small, cheap variety. At a given time one of the ringleaders sent a marble through the nearest pane of glass. That was the signal, and from all sides came the cracking of glass as one after another took up the mischievous work. In vain the prefect watched; by a deft movement of the fingers a marble could be propelled with sufficient force to break a pane of glass, and the movement so concealed as to make discovery almost impossible. This was kept up that night in the dormitory and next day in the class-rooms, study-hall, and refectory, until there was hardly a pane of glass in the house left unbroken. But, as is usual in such cases, the ringleaders were discovered and summarily expelled, and the other offenders were promised immunity from punishment, if each would report to the treasurer how many panes he had broken, in order that he might be obliged to pay for them. The quaking conspirators gladly availed themselves of this opportunity, and escaped further punishment.

The Cæcilia Society at that time gave frequent musical entertainments, the most important of which was
generally given on Evacuation day, November 25th,
and Father Larkin introduced the custom of giving
musical and literary entertainments on Washington's
birthday, St. Patrick's day, and St. John the Baptist's
day. It will be seen, therefore, how unfounded were
the opinions of the boys on his alleged prejudice.

During Father Larkin's presidency the Know-Nothing troubles were at their height. Two meetings were
held on Fordham Heights for the purpose of organizing
to burn the college. A Mr. Cole, a blacksmith on the
Kingsbridge road, threatened to expose the plot if they
did not desist, and the attack on the college was frus-
trated. At this time the government furnished the
college with twelve muskets for the better defence of
the institution. These muskets lay around until the
beginning of the civil war, when one of a number of
boys who were playing with the arms was stabbed in
the groin by a bayonet, and the guns were then put
away out of reach. In later years they became the
property of the Dramatic Association, and figured in
many a performance on the college boards. Some of
them are still to be found in the Property Room of the
Dramatic Association. November 3, 1853, the Papal
Legate, Monsignore Bedini, visited the college with
Bishop Hughes and the Bishop of Brooklyn, and a reception was tendered them by the students.

Father Larkin was president until 1854, and throughout his entire term was a great favorite with the boys.
It is probable that no member of the faculty since the
founding of the college ever acquired such an extraordinary influence over the students of all ages as did

Father Larkin, and there was no one, perhaps, whose memory has been so faithfully cherished by his old pupils as that of this handsome, genial Englishman. And this wonderful attachment was not on the part of the students alone. The prefects and teachers had just as strong a regard for him. "I know," adds Mr. Hassard, "that Father Gockeln almost worshipped the ground he trod upon."

During Father Larkin's last year as president, Father Gockeln arrived from Canada and succeeded Father Ouellet as Prefect of Discipline. The change was a welcome one to the boys, for Father Ouellet's methods of enforcing discipline were severe, almost to harshness. He was an excellent disciplinarian, but one whose manner and course of action were likely to render him very unpopular. Later he taught in the Commercial course, or "Purgatory," as it was commonly called, where he had as a pupil James McMahon, afterward Colonel James McMahon, who served with such distinction and was killed in the civil war. He was a brother of General Martin T. McMahon, '55, who, with Hassard and Arthur Francis, founded and managed the *Goose-Quill*, the first journalistic effort that Fordham had ever known. The *Goose-Quill*, of which we shall say more in its proper place, was started during Father Larkin's term as president, but not with his entire approval. He was very conservative and abhorred newspapers; he would not allow them to have it printed.

Many years later, when the call of duty summoned Father Ouellet to the bloody scenes of the civil war, he acted well his part. He was chaplain of the Sixty-ninth New York Regiment, and was always found where the dying lay closest, where the danger was greatest, caring nothing for himself and endangering his life at every movement. There were others, too, of the Fordham fathers who went to the front in those trying times, and won renown (and something more) by their bravery and self-sacrifice. "Father Nash," says General McMahon, "did more to discipline Billy Wilson's Zouaves than all their officers." Father Tissot, who was acting president of Fordham in 1864 and '65, was another who distinguished himself in that unhappy struggle, and by his bravery and devotion at Antietam attracted the attention of General Hancock.

These are, to a certain extent, digressions, as the incidents detailed happened at a much later period than that of which we are treating, but they are subjects in which Fordham should glory, and therefore worthy of place in these pages.

Let us return therefore to our story. One afternoon before the close of Father Larkin's term, the usual stillness of the study hour was broken by the entrance of the president accompanied by a strange gentleman. Proceeding to the platform at the end of the study-hall, he introduced the stranger as the distinguished Irish patriot, Thomas Francis Meagher, who had just escaped from penal servitude in Van Diemen's Land, whither he had been sentenced for his devotion to the cause of his country. He spoke to the assembled students, on the subject that was nearest to his heart, with that warmth and fervor, that fiery eloquence that made him one of the most fascinating and magnetic orators of his day. In connection with this address a story is told of the Reverend Thomas J. Mooney, then a student in the college, but now many years deceased.

Father Mooney was a native of Birmingham, England, and as the boys passed out of the hall at the close of Meagher's impassioned harangue, he turned to a friend, Mr. Joseph Kinney, of New York, and remarked that he never was ashamed of being an Englishman until that day, but such was the effect of Meagher's burning words, his vivid picture of the wrongs of his country, that the Englishman was obliged to blush for the land of his nativity. Mr. Kinney, from whom we have this incident, recalls another notable event that happened about the same time, a visit and address by that other distinguished Irishman, Father Theobald Mathew. Father Mathew addressed the boys in the same study-hall, and concluded his remarks by asking for a holiday, which was promptly granted.

Among the students of that period the most notable was undoubtedly the late John R. G. Hassard, '55, the distinguished journalist, who died in the spring of 1888. His career in college was one of unqualified success. He was revered by fellow-students and professors alike; by the latter he was looked upon as a young man of more than ordinary uprightness and steadiness, while among the boys his influence for good was truly wonderful. He was an ardent lover of music and literature, and even before his graduation had become a master of English style. Shortly after his graduation he was appointed one of the writers on the "American Encyclopædia," and was rapidly advanced by Messrs. Ripley and Dana until he became managing editor. He was later private secretary to Mr. Dana and associated with him in several journalistic ventures. In his last years he was connected with the New York *Tribune* as musical critic.

Mr. Hassard, General Martin T. McMahon, and Arthur Francis, all of the class of '55, were the editors of the *Goose-Quill*, of which mention has several times been made in this work. Arthur Francis died shortly after graduation, and the only surviving member of the editorial staff of the *Goose-Quill*, and, indeed, of that whole class, is General McMahon. Mr. Thomas B. Connery, who was for many years editor-in-chief of the New York *Herald*, and was afterward secretary to the American Legation at Mexico, was graduated in '53; and the Reverend Dr. Richard Brennan, A.M., '54, a well-known divine of the archdiocese of New York, was among those who received their degrees at this time.

In 1852, the Reverend Louis Jouin, S.J., a famous philosopher, mathematician, and linguist, and now the venerable professor of philosophy in the post-graduate course, came to Fordham and took charge of a class in mathematics, in which were Mr. Hassard, General McMahon, and other well-known men. Father Jouin was later appointed vice-president. He is the author of several text-books which are now in use at Fordham and many other colleges. His "Logic and Metaphysics," "Moral Philosophy," and "Evidences of Religion," have each reached a fourth edition. Monsignor Bernard O'Reilly, who has since left the order, was a member of the faculty of Fordham for a number of years, having been professor of belles-lettres under Father Larkin.

CHAPTER IX.

In 1854 the presidency of Fordham passed from Father Larkin to the Reverend Remigius Tellier. Few changes were made in the outward appearance of the college during the latter's term of office, which lasted until 1860; and such as were made pertained to the domestic department, and are not therefore of vital interest. In 1855 the Mathematical course was arranged as follows: in classics, algebra was taught; in belles-lettres, geometry and trigonometry; in rhetoric, the second part of trigonometry and analytical geometry; and in philosophy, the second part of analytical geometry and mechanics. The following year calculus was added to the course. The semi-annual examinations were inaugurated this year, one in February and one in June; and a third division of the students was established. This was, as now, for very young boys, and occupied the building corresponding to the "castle," in which are now the shoe shop and bakery.

But the most important event that took place under Father Tellier's presidency was the founding of the St. John's Debating Society. This organization was established in 1854.

Under the constitution the president was appointed

REV. REMIGIUS TELLIER, S.J.
a Paris

by the faculty, and was generally, although not neces-
sarily so, the professor of rhetoric. The other officers
were selected by ballot. On the first board of officers we find the Reverend M. C. Smarius, S.J., president, General McMahon, vice-president, and Mr. Hassard, secretary. The Crimean war was uppermost in
men's minds at that time, and the question debated at
the first meeting was, "Were the Western powers, as
Christian nations, justified in espousing the cause of the
Turks?" The spirit with which the members entered
into the discussion may be judged from the fact that
the debate lasted through three or four sessions, and
was marked by earnest and enthusiastic work.

Rose Hill rejoiced in those days in a choir that had
attained a high degree of proficiency. Under the lead-
ership of Mr. Hector Glackmeyer, S.J., assisted by Mr.
Doucet, afterward Father Doucet, president of the
college, and Brother Julius Macé, it had acquired such
familiarity with music that the most difficult composi-
tions were not beyond its endeavor. Mr. Glackmeyer
and Mr. Doucet were accomplished and cultivated singers, and Brother Macé was an organist and pianist of
rare talent and ability. He was a pupil of the famous
Bertini, and a fellow-student and intimate friend of
Gottschalk.

It is said that on one occasion, when the latter was
performing before a large and admiring audience, he
was secretly informed that his old friend Brother
Macé was present in the hall. He immediately came
forward and announced that there was one present
whose talents he considered superior to his own; he
begged his friend to set aside his wonted modesty
and come forward to take his, the speaker's, place. At

this point several of the audience noticed Brother Macé nervously making his way toward the street, and, although they had never seen him before, suspected that he was the gentleman to whom the great musician referred. They stopped him in spite of his protests, and the attention of the entire audience was attracted. Remonstrance was now in vain, and amid the plaudits of the multitude the humble lay-brother of the Society of Jesus was escorted to the platform, where he was soon playing to the delight of a ravished audience.

A strong attachment existed between the saintly brother and his old master, and after the death of the former, in 1889, a valuable souvenir of their friendship was found among his papers. It was an autograph copy of one of Beethoven's sonatas, with annotations by Bertini, which had been presented by the latter to his favorite pupil.

Brother Macé was a native of Nantes, the chief town of the Loire-Inférieure. He was born in 1822, and entered the Jesuit novitiate, as a lay-brother, in 1847. He came to America the following year, and the subsequent forty-one years of his life were spent at Fordham.

Journalism at St. John's did not entirely die out with the demise of the *Goose-Quill*, which occurred in 1855 or 1856. Several efforts were made to revive the spirit, but they were futile. *Sem, The Collegian*, and a less pretentious sheet published on Second Division, called *The Spy*, in turn sprang into existence, sickened, and died, and then the spirit of journalism lay dormant for over twenty years.

But another event of considerable importance took

place during the presidency of Father Tellier, an event which is of more interest to the average college student than the struggles of ambitious journalists. We refer to the organization of the college base-ball team. It was the first step toward an organized athletic association, and for many years the only field of athletics in which Fordham was represented. Cricket and "rounders" had been favorite pastimes, but as base-ball grew in public favor, the other sports lost ground and were gradually dropped. For years the new game was played without any attempt at organization, but it was before a movement was started in that direction. The first regular team was organized September 13, 1859, under the name of the Rose Hill Base-ball Club, the college at that time being generally known as Rose Hill College. The first game was played on November 3, 1859, with a team from St. Francis Xavier's College, New York. The score at the end of the sixth inning was 33-11, in favor of Rose Hill.

In 1857 the first dramatic entertainment of any pretensions was given in the study-hall by the members of the Classes of Belles-lettres and Classics. A programme of this entertainment is in the possession of the Dramatic Association.

The attendance at the college was slowly increasing, year by year, and in 1856 there were nearly two hundred students in the house. Among the graduates of 1860 we find the name of Winand M. Wigger, now Bishop of Newark, N. J. Three years before General James R. O'Beirne received his diploma; and in 1857, the Rev. Dr. Henry A. Brann, of New York, was added to the ranks of the Fordham graduates. General McMahon, Mr. Hassard, Arthur Francis, the

7

Rev. James L. Conron, all of the class of '55; Mr. Joseph J. Marvin, '58, and Mr. Peter A. Hargous, '57, were also among those graduated under Father Tellier.

In 1859, one year before Father Tellier's retirement from the presidency, the first of the prizes · for the graduating class was established. In that year Archbishop Hughes founded the medal for the best biographical essay. It is of gold, worth fifty dollars, and is donated every year by some friend of the college. The following year, 1860, Father Tellier, after filling the office of president for six years, retired, and Father Thébaud was reappointed for another term to the office he had left vacant nine years before. This, his second term, was marked by several events of importance. In September, 1860, the second year of philosophy, or post-graduate course, was instituted, and the Seminary building and church purchased from Archbishop Hughes for $85,000. The same year a marble quarry in Tremont was purchased by the college, and a blue-stone quarry was opened in the woods near the Bronx. These two quarries have supplied the material for all the buildings, except the new Faculty building, that have been erected since that time. About this time an addition was made to the college property by the purchase of a portion of the Powell farm. This farm was an estate that adjoined Rose Hill on the south, and at the time of the accession of the Jesuits to the college the Powell farm-house was the only building in sight. It had been occupied until a short time previous as a school for young men, conducted by the Reverend Mr. Powell, an Episcopalian minister, but had been closed. When the Jesuits took possession of the college, Father Thébaud was anxious to purchase a portion of the Powell property, but his superiors did not consider it advisable to increase the debt, and the project was abandoned. Later, however, when the property was placed on the market, it was deemed advisable to negotiate for the purchase, and consequently the lower part of the lawn was extended to what is now Pelham Avenue.

In 1861 Father Thébaud built a three-story wooden house, with curb roof and odd-looking dormer windows, at the rear of the refectory wing and on the edge of the garden. This building was devoted to the use of Third Division, the recreation-room being on the first floor, the study-hall on the second, and the top floor being presumably used as a dormitory. At right angles with this building, adjoining the southern end and separating Second and Third Divisions, was the one-story wooden building that formerly extended back from the central stone building. It will be remembered that during Father Thébaud's first term this building was removed and a three-story brick extension erected which is still standing.

In 1862 the gatekeeper's lodge was built. It has been said that it was built as an experiment to test the endurance of the stone supplied by the newly opened quarry in the woods. That the test was satisfactory needs no further assurance than the fact that the four college buildings since erected have been made of the same material.

Father Thébaud's next care was for the improvement of the approach from the gate to the college buildings. We have already seen that the grounds were shaded by numbers of venerable elms. Father Thébaud laid out the avenues as they are to-day, and planted young trees in such a way that they lined both avenues from the gate to the entrance of the main building.

On March 26, 1862, the St. John's Historical Association was established. The object of the association is to encourage historical research and promote the investigation and diffusion of historical truth. The moderator is appointed by the faculty, and the other officers are elected semi-annually.

We now reach a period in the history of St. John's which is interesting in many ways, but particularly from the association with the college and its professors of that most unfortunate and most maligned of men, and most fascinating of poets, Edgar Allan Poe.

The period we refer to is that of the latter part of Father Thébaud's term of office, and that of his successor, Father Doucet. This gentleman was a famous musician and a preacher of no mean ability, to whom we have more than once referred in these pages. He succeeded Father Thébaud in the latter part of 1863. He was a close friend of poor Poe, who loved to wander about the college grounds and mingle with the fathers, with all of whom he was on terms of the closest intimacy.

" I knew him well," said Father Doucet, on one occasion. "In bearing and countenance he was extremely refined. His features were somewhat sharp and very thoughtful. He was well informed on all matters. I always thought he was a gentleman by nature and instinct."

Father Doucet always indignantly denied the statement so freely made that Poe looked like one worn out by dissipation and excess. The unfortunate poet had one weakness, a weakness that amounted almost to a

Rev. EDWARD DOUCET, S.J.

8TH PRESIDENT.

malady, but against which he fought manfully and well.
Poor Poe ! His enemies, for he had many, made cap-
ital out of his weakness, and hounded him with an
animosity and a persistency that would have broken
a less sturdy spirit.

Father Doucet did not long continue to exercise the
functions of president.   At the end of his first year he
was called away to Europe, and his duties then devolved on the vice-president, the Reverend Peter Tissot.
At the end of another year it became necessary to make
a change, and Father Tissot was retired and the Reverend William Moylan, S.J., appointed in his stead.

CHAPTER X.

FATHER MOYLAN, the new president, was a native of Ireland, and had come to this country at an early age. Before his admission to the Society he had done a great deal of missionary work as a secular priest among the Indians and the fishermen at Cape Gaspé, on the shores of the Gulf of St. Lawrence. On November 14, 1851, at the age of twenty-nine, he was admitted to the order and assigned to teach in the under-graduate course at Fordham, after which he was sent to St. Francis Xavier's, in West Sixteenth Street, New York, and subsequently to San Francisco. In 1865 he was appointed president at Fordham.

Father Moylan was in many respects a remarkable man. His ability as a teacher was well known, and he was ranked among the foremost preachers of the time, the vigor and eloquence of his sermons having won for him years before an enviable position among the pulpit orators of the day. His appointment was a source of great pleasure to Archbishop Hughes, who esteemed him very highly. He was austere, stern, and rigorous in the discharge of his duties, whatever they might be or wherever they might call him. He had an oddity of manner that amounted almost to eccentricity, but he was conscientious to the last degree, and never once swerved a hair's-breadth from the straight

Rev. JOSEPH SHEA, S.J.
10TH PRESIDENT.

and narrow way he had laid out for himself. He was no time-server, and rich and poor, high and low were all the same to him. His whole life was a model of firmness and consistency. The virtues that he preached from the altar and inculcated in the confessional he devotedly practised in his private life. He was sharp and somewhat irritable in manner, but beneath his brusque exterior there beat a true and kindly heart. The end came to him on the scene of his former labors. He died peacefully and quietly at Fordham, January 14, 1891, nearly forty years after his entrance into the Society. He was buried in the college cemetery.

The chief monument that Father Moylan has left after him at Fordham is the Senior Hall, or First Division building, which was finished under his supervision. This was the first of the college buildings built of the blue stone and marble from the lately acquired quarries, and was for many years the principal college building.

The new building was finished in the summer of 1867. It is a four-story building with mansard roof, containing the gymnasium, reading and billiard-rooms, study-hall, and dormitories of the Senior Division.

Father Moylan evidently intended this new building simply as a part of an extensive plan, for the end wall which faced the lawn was left in an unfinished state. Something interfered with his plans, as the structure was not completed, and the rough wall remained until the new faculty building, erected in 1890, hid it from view.

In 1868 Father Moylan having served for the short term of three years, but having accomplished a world of good in that time, was replaced by Reverend Joseph Shea.

As we come nearer to the present day we become
more interested, owing to the fact that we are dealing
with those whose names are still on our lips and whose
deeds are still green in the memory of living men. Like
the others, Father Shea took up the work at the point
at which it was dropped by his predecessor, the
machinery of the institution moving evenly as before and never slipping a cog. Father Shea's chief
contribution toward the outer embellishment of the
college was the removal of the two one-story wings
of the central building, and the erection in their stead
of the wings that now stand. In the south wing, where
the study-hall had been, the students' chapel is now lo-
cated on the first floor and the rooms of the professors
in the upper portion. When the new chapel in the faculty building (finished this summer) is ready for occupation, the present place of worship will be used as
music-rooms.

To the old student who has so often knelt in worship in the little old chapel, it will seem like desecra-
tion to have other and profane sounds heard within
those walls that seem continually to vibrate to the
choir's inspiring strains of the mass and the solemn
measures of many a well-known hymn or canticle. But
there remains this grain of consolation, that the chapel
is devoted to a cause which, though less sublime, is not
a degradation of the sacred place. It will be sacred
to the genius of music.

The north wing still serves the purpose originally
designed for its predecessor. The students' refectory,
which occupied the old building, is now found on the
first floor of the edifice erected by Father Shea, while
the community refectory is on the second floor. An

accident occurred during the erection of this building which, although it did no injury to life or limb, was yet most unfortunate. In the spring of 1869, while the workmen were digging along the foundation of the old refectory in order to lay the foundation for the new building, the side walls and roof caved in. Fortunately the students had just left the room and no one was injured, though considerable damage was done otherwise. Provision has been made, however, in the new faculty building, for a refectory for students, as also one for the community, and when these are completed the present refectory will then be given over to the military and become a drill-room and armory.

Father Shea ruled the old institution for six years, until 1874. The position of president at the period at which he occupied it was a very trying one. The authorities had determined to try the effect of a change in the methods of management of the college, and for a time the discipline was relaxed and the loose manner of secular institutions prevailed at Fordham. The system was given a fair trial during Father Shea's term, but it was found to be a failure and abandoned.

During the later years of Father Shea's term, among the additions to the faculty was one who has become a most prominent figure in the later history of the college, and whose name will never be forgotten by any Fordhamite of the '70 to '80 period. Reverend Thomas J. A. Freeman in the summer of 1872 stepped into the charge of the Scientific department, and from that time until 1889, with the exception of a few years at intervals spent in other colleges, reigned supreme over the classes of physics and chemistry.

When Father Freeman arrived at Fordham the

Scientific department was not in a flourishing condition. The Classes of Physics and Chemistry were then held in adjoining rooms in the old building that connected the chapel wing with the "castle;" the latter building was, it may be stated, torn down last summer.

Early in 1872 the Scientific department was moved to the old seminary, now St. John's Hall, which had been sold to the college in 1860, as we have already stated. The entire first floor, now occupied by the study-hall, music and reading-rooms, was cleared and elaborately fitted up. It was a welcome change from the close quarters the classes had hitherto been obliged to content themselves with. The rooms were large and airy, and afforded ample facilities for the proper disposal of the museum, physical apparatus, etc. The upper floors were turned into rooms for the seniors, and the small room in the basement, now used for a billiard-room for the small boys, was occupied by the class of philosophy. When this class moved, a short time afterward, to the First Division building, Father Freeman took possession of the room as a workshop. Here he repaired the old instruments—many of which had come from Kentucky in the early days of the college—and made many new ones. The Scientific department remained here until 1886, when the new Science Hall, begun by Father Dealy, was completed by his successor, Father Campbell.

The younger generation of students of this period has not yet had time to rise to the prominence attained by those of an earlier day; yet already all the graduates of the '60's and '70's have risen to places of honor and distinction in the various walks of life. Several have been especially honored, as Reverend

REV. F. W. GOCKELN, S.J.
IITH PRESIDENT.

Charles F. H. O'Neill, '74, who died in 1888 at Peoria, Ill. He had been appointed two years before to the position of pastor to the cathedral in Peoria, and a short time later was raised to the dignity of chancellor of the diocese. Morgan J. O'Brien, '72, of this city, who graduated in 1872, was chosen by the Democratic party in 1887 as their candidate for judge of the Supreme Court of the State of New York, and elected by a large majority, and has worn the ermine of his office without reproach. Among others was Edward Bermudez, A.M., '74, of New Orleans, La., who has also risen to the bench; Joaquin Arrita, '71, who was in this country in the fall of 1889 as secretary to the representative of San Salvador to the Pan-American Congress then in session, and John B. Shea, '74, of Fordham, who creditably served a term in the State Legislature at Albany and has filled other public positions since.

In July, 1874, Father Shea retired from the presidency and made way for Reverend F. William Gockeln, whose arrival at St. Mary's, Ky., and subsequent appointment as vice-president at Fordham we have already noticed. At the close of the term of vice-president, in 1869, Father Gockeln was ordered to Woodstock, Md., where he remained one year. From there he went to Guelph, Ont., and thence to St. Lawrence's Rectory, in New York City, as superior, and thence, in the summer of 1874, to Fordham, to assume the heavy responsibility and arduous duties of President of St. John's College. And these duties were rendered particularly arduous at that time by a combination of circumstances that requires some explanation. The lax system of discipline introduced under the *régime* of Father Shea had been fairly tried and found wanting, and although the number of students had increased the college suffered in reputation.

Such was the state of affairs when Father Gockeln arrived in Fordham. He was not long in grasping the situation, and once grasped, in meeting and grappling with the obstacles to progress which it created. He saw there was a need for prompt, immediate, and vigorous action, and he did not hesitate a moment in deciding what his course should be. He was not a man to employ half-way measures, but, on the contrary, was a believer in heroic treatment and radical methods for the rooting out of evil, and these he immediately adopted. By his first official act he restored the former strict discipline, re-established the rules that had been in force in former years, and gave early notice and ample warning that these rules would be rigidly enforced. The time was ripe for action, and he seized upon it. The change was naturally a sudden one, but the students were soon brought to a proper realization of the situation and acquiesced in the new order of things with good grace. Within six months all trace of the former laxity had passed away, and the reputation of the college rapidly rose once more.

In spite of his radical policy and seemingly severe methods of government, the new rector soon found his way to the hearts of the students. He was a man well calculated to win the love, respect, and admiration of all who came in contact with him. Genial and hearty, the soul of good-nature, scholarly, and with refinement and nobility stamped on every feature of his splendid face, he was indeed a man among men. Father Halpin, now vice-president of St. John's, who was associated with him for so many years, says of him: "He was a

large-souled, big-hearted man; he was loyal and devoted.   I have seen tears in his eyes when he spoke of
the Society of Jesus.   How he resented any calumny
against it!   How he grew eloquent as he spoke its
praises!   He sank himself in his calling.   There was
no sacrifice he did not court for its sake.   He was a
true child of obedience, as all his superiors attest.   His
was a bright and a pure life, and still, much as he naturally abhorred contact with men whose lives were
branded with certain crimes, his hand was ever out-
stretched to lift them up from their degradation.   His
sympathy was boundless.   He gave ear to every tale
of distress, and rendered every assistance at his command."

St. John's soon regained its former position, the number of students increased, and although no outward improvements in the way of erection of new buildings
were accomplished, the studies advanced under Father
Gockeln and the able corps of professors who assisted
him in the management.   •

Among the most prominent of those associated with
Father Gockeln in the work at St. John's was Reverend P. O. Racicot, who was professor of philosophy
during the first year of Father Gockeln's presidency,
and was later vice-president and chief disciplinarian.
Father Racicot was born in Montreal in 1839.   He was
educated at the Sulpician Seminary and entered the
Jesuit Order in 1855.   Nearly twenty years of his life
as a Jesuit were spent at Fordham.   He had a wonderful memory, a sound, clear judgment, and was an indefatigable worker.   He died in Boston, March 27 (Good
Friday), 1891.   The *Fordham Monthly* of April, 1891,
says of him :

" Father Racicot was one of the most self-contained and warmest-hearted men that ever breathed. He was strict, it is true, and firm when serious faults had to be corrected under his guidance and direction, but withal he was most kindly and generous. How many there are, boys and men, who have experienced his great kindness and even affection."

In 1877 the office of vice-president was filled by the Reverend John Treanor, who accompanied the family of ex-Judge Charles Donohue to the Pacific coast, and who was killed by an accident on the way. Reverend Nicholas Hanrahan, whose connection with the college extended over a period of more than thirty years, and who died in April, 1891, was treasurer; and in other positions we find Father Doucet, once president, but now a subordinate; Reverend P. Cassidy, now president of St. Peter's, Jersey City; the present president of St. John's, Father Scully, and Father Halpin, now vice-president. In 1882, after presiding eight years over the destinies of the college, Father Gockeln was sent by his superiors to Holy Cross College, Worcester, Mass.; from there to Jersey City, and thence to Providence, R. I., where he died early in 1887.

REV. P. F. DEALY, S.J

12TH PRESIDENT.

CHAPTER XI.

THE accession of Reverend P. F. Dealy to the presidency in 1882, marks the beginning of a new era in the history of Fordham College; a transition from the conservative opinions of the Jesuits of the old French school to the broader and more liberal ideas which have begun to spread as the older generation of fathers is passing away. We have already alluded to the old French idea of removing seminaries and colleges as far as possible from large cities, and, as is urged in favor of the system, equally far from the temptations of the world. The fallacy of this idea is so apparent now, and it has been so generally repudiated, that it is hardly necessary to dwell on it here. Looked at from a financial stand-point, the lack of wisdom of the scheme cannot but be readily perceptible at the first glance, and if proof is wanted we may find it in the fact that institutions so situated, whatever advantages they may possess, never rise above the rank of obscure academies, with little or no prestige, and utterly unknown outside the narrow circle of their graduates and students.

Although Fordham was not thus geographically isolated from the world, or buried beyond the ken of the general public, the old spirit was still in the ascendant, and reared such a wall of conservatism around the institution that, to all intents and purposes, it was miles away from the heart of the great city of which it was a part.   And the first to break down this barrier and open the way for freer intercourse with the outer world was Father Dealy.

He was not without a thorough acquaintance with Fordham College, its manners and customs.   In September, 1843, nearly fifty years ago, he was one of the students, and later he entered the Jesuit novitiate also at Fordham.   He was not slow, therefore, in showing his progressive spirit, and one of the first signs of advancement was the establishment of a College paper.   For many years there had been a strong need for such a publication, but since the days of the *Goose-Quill* and *Sem* no effort had been made in this direction until November, 1882, when the first number of the *Fordham College Monthly* made its appearance.

In the matter of improving the college surroundings Father Dealy did much.   He laid macadamized roads, each bordered by a flagged pathway from the entrance gate to the college and the church, respectively.   He also beautified the lawn, and materially improved the outward appearance of the college, and had the little church entirely refitted and handsomely frescoed.

The next step was the repairing of the old seminary building, which for years had been going to ruin. It was used at the time only for the Science classes, and had been allowed slowly to fall into decay.   The drainage had been neglected, the adjoining ground had become overgrown with weeds, and was strewn with decaying vegetation, and everything about the handsome old building showed evidence of neglect; yet, even in the midst of its wretched surroundings, it stood out the most picturesque piece of architecture on the college property.   Father Dealy had plans in view for utilizing the old building which he put into operation.   A donation of $5,000 from the estate of the Reverend F. X. McGovern, S.J., furnished him with the means for the needed improvements.   The building was remodelled, the drainage improved, and the interior rendered dry, safe, and healthy as any house on the ground.   The plot in front of the building was cleared of its noxious vegetation, gravelled walks laid out, fences and hedges repaired, and the whole restored in such a way as to make it " a thing of beauty," and an attraction to the college.   Into the remodelled seminary he moved the dormitories and some of the classrooms of the boys of the Preparatory department, and it then became known as St. John's Hall.   The study-hall, recreation-rooms, and play-ground of the small boys still remained at the old place, the two first in the curb-roofed building that was built for the purpose by Father Thébaud.   The change was needed, as the latter building was fast becoming useless for school purposes.   Father Dealy then began making arrangements for the transfer of the Scientific department in order to make room in the Seminary for the entire Preparatory school.   With this end in view, a site for a new building was selected about eighty yards south of the Senior Hall, and plans were prepared for a building which would furnish accommodation for the Classes of Physics and Chemistry, for the library, the four highest classes, and the engine-room.   To connect the last-named room with the other buildings a tunnel was constructed through which the pipes from the boilers would pass to the various buildings.

8

In the summer of 1885 ground was broken for this tunnel, but the work was but fairly under way when Father Dealy was removed, and the task of completing Science Hall and its subterranean connection was left to his successor, the Reverend Thomas J. Campbell, S.J. Another achievement, the credit of which belongs to Father Dealy, but the fruit of which was not borne until after he had resigned his trust, was the introduction of military instruction into the curriculum of the college.

It was a fortunate circumstance for the institution that when Father Dealy resigned his post his mantle fell on the shoulders of a man who, though much younger and less experienced, had the courage, energy, and progressive spirit which promised rapid advancement for the college. The Reverend Thomas J. Campbell, his successor, now Provincial of the New York-Maryland province, is a man whose scholarly attainments and executive ability are conceded by all who know him. During his term of three years at Fordham the standard of scholarship rapidly advanced, and the tone and character of the various associations, and even of the students themselves, seemed to have been elevated under his influence.

The military drill, which, as we have already stated, had just been introduced, had become a prominent feature of the course of instruction; and though at first most of the students were chary about entering the company, that feeling subsequently yielded to the beneficial influence of the "new departure." For instructor they had an enthusiastic and energetic young officer, Lieutenant Herbert G. Squiers, of the Seventh U. S. Cavalry, who spared no pains to make the company

Rev. THOMAS CAMPBELL, S.J.

13TH PRESIDENT.

a credit to the college—a devotion which was rewarded
in the end by a success as complete and unqualified as
it was deserved.   Taking a dozen of the most promis-
ing students as a nucleus of his corps, he organized before the close of the year a well-drilled, handsome company of nearly fifty.   The organization rapidly gained
favor, and through the efforts of its energetic preceptor
grew until it is now one of the most attractive features
of the college course.

Under Father Campbell a notable change took place
in the management of the Debating Society.   Disap-
proving of the old system by which the speeches of
the debaters were carefully written and committed to
memory in anticipation of the debate, he inaugurated a
plan which, though new to Fordham, had been tried in
other colleges.   He had the meetings of the society carried on after the plan of the British House of Commons, measures being brought up and debated in strict
parliamentary form.   By this means Father Campbell
hoped to cultivate extempore speaking, and to develop
the faculty of thinking on one's feet.   This change
took place in the fall of 1886, and in the following
year a similar change was made in the operations
of St. John's Literary Society, formed of the higher
classes in the Commercial course.   This was changed
to the House of Representatives, and business was
carried on as in the lower house of the United States
Congress.

The Science Hall, which was begun by Father Dealy
in the spring of 1885, was completed in 1886, and in
September of that year was opened for use by Father
Campbell.   It is an ornamental building of two stories,
with slate roof and tall, graceful chimney at the west-

ern end, and is built of the same description of stone as
is used in Senior Hall. In the same year the Third
Division, or Preparatory school, was moved to St. John's
Hall, and in 1887 the grounds at the rear thereof were
terraced. The shed which occupied the place of the
present music-room in 1846, and which was moved by
Father Thébaud to the line between Second and Third
Divisions, was torn down and removed in the summer
of 1886, and the old Third Division building turned
into a shop and storehouse. The year 1886–87 was
marked by many other incidents worthy of note.
The Scientific course with the surveying class, and the
classes of English, philosophy, and rhetoric were established. The bronze statue of the Blessed Virgin, which
stood in the centre of the quadrangle until the latter
was invaded by the new Faculty building, was unveiled
with impressive ceremonies on February 2, 1887, the
anniversary of the founding of the Parthenian Sodality,
and was solemnly blessed on May 1st of the same year.
A specially distinctive feature of this year was, that it
was one of unprecedented success for athletics of all
kinds—the Base-Ball Nine having made a record that
has never been rivalled, except perhaps by the team of
1890. The Dramatic Society of that year was unusu-
ally successful, and the experiment in the Debating
Society was in every way satisfactory.

The following year (1887–88) was the last of Father
Campbell's term, and during its course he introduced
electric lights into the college. A dynamo was placed
in the cellar of Science Hall, and the First and Second
Division study-halls, and the students' and community
refectories were lighted by incandescent lamps. The
stage in the First Division hall was also lighted by

LANE (NEAR SKATING-POND) LEADING TO BRONX PARK.

electricity, and so arranged that the lights could be raised or lowered at will.

In May, 1888, the news reached Fordham that Father Campbell had been raised to the dignity of Provincial of the New York-Maryland province.   The sorrow caused by the announcement of his retirement from the presidency was general among the students, and the knowledge that he had been called away to greater honors and a position of higher dignity was hardly sufficient to reconcile them to the loss of so popular a rector.

The elevation of Father Campbell to the office of Provincial left a vacancy at Fordham which was filled the following summer by the appointment of Reverend John Scully, the present incumbent.   Father Scully, who is a son of Edward Scully, of Sandy Hill, N. Y., was born in Brooklyn, N. Y., in 1846, but was educated at private schools in Albany.   In 1872 he entered the Society of Jesus, making his novitiate in Canada, his rhetoric studies at Roehampton, England, and his philosophical studies at Stonyhurst.   In 1878 he was sent to Fordham as a professor, and later to Georgetown College.   After his ordination he became prefect of studies at St. Peter's College, Jersey City, and in July, 1888, he was appointed to the vacant presidency of St. John's, Fordham.

Among Father Scully's first official acts was the sale of the property on the banks of the Bronx to the city of New York.   This property is a beautiful bit of woodland extending from the Southern Boulevard to the Bronx River, presenting at every turn of its winding paths some charming view of the river seen through interlocking boughs and tangled brushwood.   It is an ideal spot, and its advantages were soon discovered by the city authorities when the establishment of Bronx Park was first proposed. The purchase was completed in 'April, 1889, the city paying $93,966.25 for the property. It is near this spot that the Botanical Gardens are to be established.

About this time the question of a statue to Archbishop Hughes was mooted and the occasion selected as the most appropriate, the Commencement-day of 1889, the twenty-fifth anniversary of the archbishop's death having occurred during that year. The matter was held in abeyance for the time being, however, and the date for the erection of the statue was postponed until the jubilee celebration in 1891.

Ever since he took the reins of government at Fordham in his hands, Father Scully had been planning new buildings which had been sorely needed for many years. By the fall of 1889 his plans had matured, and in the early part of December of that year, ground was broken for the new Junior Hall, or Second Division building. It was a much needed improvement. The old Second Division building, which had been standing nearly fifty years, was fast becoming unfit for use, and the increasing attendance caused a demand for better accommodation.

The site of the new building was on the old Third Division recreation ground, and the removal of the old frame building erected by Father Thébaud for Third Division became necessary. Since the small boys had vacated it for more commodious quarters in St. John's Hall, the old house had been put to a variety of uses. The ground floor had been turned into a stationery shop, presided over by one of the lay-brothers; the second floor, the old study-hall, had become the armory, and the top floor, quarters for some of the servants. But its day was over, it stood in the way of progress, and there was but one course left, it must be removed. So the old relic disappeared, and, phœnix-like, out of its ashes rose the handsome new Junior Hall. This edifice, which was completed in 1890, is in general outline identical with the Senior Hall built by Father Moylan. It is of the same quality of stone, and is finished in hard wood. The gymnasium, reading-room, and billiard-room are on the first floor; the study-hall and vice-president's office on the second; the office having been moved from the First Division building on the completion of the newer edifice. The third and fourth stories are occupied as class-rooms and the dormitory, respectively. On the top floor are the rooms occupied by the members of the Class of Philosophy.

Before this building was completed Father Scully had begun the erection of another, in the form of an extension to the Senior Hall, at the point left unfinished for that purpose by Father Moylan. Foundations were laid for a building to meet the old hall at right angles, to be one hundred and seventy feet in length, by about fifty feet in width. On Sunday, August 16th, the same year, the corner-stone of the new Faculty building, for it is intended chiefly for the rooms of the fathers and scholastics, was laid by Bishop Conroy. The sermon was preached by the Reverend William A. Dunphy, '75, who has since that time been called to his account, having died in less than six months after. The silver trowel used on this occasion was the gift of Mr. Paul Thébaud, who was a student at the college early in the forties. The first and second stories of the north end will be occupied as a beautiful new chapel for the students; on the corresponding floors in the southern end will be the refectories, and above will be the rooms of the professors.

The same year that saw the Junior Hall completed and the new Faculty building well started on its upward way, witnessed the total destruction of two time-stained and weather-beaten relics of another era, the "castle" and the old Second Division building. The former was removed to make room for the Faculty building, and the other as it had outlived its usefulness. The laboratory of the Class of Analytical Chemistry, which was in the "castle," was moved to the Science Hall, where more suitable quarters had been prepared for it. The new laboratory contains desks and appliances for thirty-six students. This Class of Analytical Chemistry, which previous to Father Scully's presidency was confined to the Scientific course, was introduced by him into the Classical course, and is now one of the branches followed by the Senior class. The Classes of Electrical Engineering and Photography were also instituted since his accession to the presidential chair. In his second year he introduced the electric light throughout the entire institution, Father Campbell, it will be remembered, having introduced it into the refectories and study-halls. In the same year the Reverend P. A. Halpin, S.J., arrived from Boston as vice-president and prefect of studies. Father Halpin had spent many years on the faculty at Fordham College, and had been vice-president for five years under Fathers Gockeln and Dealy. He is well known throughout the country as an eloquent preacher, is the

author of a text-book used in many of the colleges, called "Precepts of Literature," and is considered one of the foremost literary men of the order.   His predecessor in the office of vice-president was Reverend George E. Quinn, a graduate of the college and an earnest worker. The Reverend Louis Jouin, the Reverend Edward Doucet, now deceased, the Reverend James P. Fagan, the Reverend Thomas J. A. Freeman, the Reverend Joseph Zwinge, the Reverend Joseph Ziegler, the Reverend Timothy O'Leary, the Reverend D. J. Mc-Goldrick, and the Reverend Lawrence Kavanagh are among those who have become identified with St. John's under Father Scully.

Among the notable events that thus far have taken place during his term of office were the golden jubilee celebrations of Father Prachensky and Brother Hennen, both of whom have since been laid away in the little cemetery.   Father Hanrahan, too, who had been a familiar figure in the treasurer's office at Fordham for many a year, was taken off quite suddenly in April, 1891.   Among the other notable men who have died at Fordham within the last few years are Fathers Moylan and Perron, Mr. Mulry, and Brothers Macé and De Pooter.

But the most important event in Father Scully's term, as, indeed, it is the most important event in the history of the college, so far, is the coming jubilee celebration.   Fordham will then celebrate the completion of her fiftieth year, and Father Scully has determined that the celebration shall be in every way a credit to the first Catholic college in the country, as Fordham can justly lay claim to be.   It is with a view to making a creditable showing on that day that the work is being hurried forward; that the matter of the statue to Archbishop Hughes has been pushed until now the unveiling on that day has been assured and the work of building the base begun.   The address of the day will be delivered by the eloquent Archbishop Ryan of Philadelphia; several of the old graduates will assist those of this year in the literary exercises, and the cadets will be marshalled in all their strength.   It will indeed be a day of triumph for St. John's.

CADET BATTALION OF ST. JOHN'S COLLEGE, FORDHAM.

CHAPTER XII.

THE CADETS.

THERE is one feature in the course of training given at Fordham which, from the prominence into which it has lately sprung and the many benefits which accrue from it, is worthy of something more than mere passing notice. The St. John's corps of cadets is a splendid body of young men, and is a credit to the institution whose name it bears. Since its organization in 1885 it has rapidly and steadily advanced, until to-day it holds the enviable position of being one of the best trained companies in the country outside of the United States Military Academy at West Point.

Were we inclined to enter deeply into a discussion of the benefits accruing from military instruction in our colleges, we might say much, for its advantages are many. But we have not at our command either the time or space for a learned disquisition on the subject. We will content ourselves, therefore, with a brief history of the military organization at Fordham from the time of its inception till the present day.

Before the establishment of the present company there had been several efforts to introduce military training into Fordham. The last of these attempts was made during the presidency of Father Gockeln and the first years of Father Dealy's rule. An ex-officer of the German army, named Bruns, was employed as instructor in military tactics, but he had no control over the students, there was no discipline, and the effort resulted in failure.

Father Dealy then set to work to obtain better facilities for carrying out his plan. He availed himself of an act of Congress which provided that United States Army officers be detailed at certain schools and colleges throughout the country, to instruct the students in military science and tactics, and after considerable work succeeded in obtaining a detail for Fordham. Although the credit of this achievement belongs to Father Dealy, he did not remain at Fordham long enough to see the new department in working order. In the catalogue of 1884–85, he announced that the necessary arrangements had been made, and that the following year would see a cadet corps at Fordham, the instructor detailed, and the arms and equipments furnished by the Government; but before the beginning of the next year he was superseded by Father Campbell.

On October 10, 1885, Lieutenant Herbert G. Squiers, of the Seventh United States Cavalry, reported for duty at Fordham, as professor of military science and tactics. Lieutenant Squiers is a pleasant, genial, young officer, but withal a strict disciplinarian and a thorough soldier. He had been appointed from civil life to a Second Lieutenancy in the First Infantry, and was afterward transferred to the Seventh Cavalry. Later, he was at the United States Artillery School at Fortress Monroe, Va., and thence was ordered to the frontier with his regiment, the Seventh Cavalry, where he remained until 1882, when he was sent to Division headquarters at Chicago, Ill. May 16, 1883, he rejoined his regiment in Dakota, where he remained until detailed to Fordham in 1885.

He immediately set to work to organize a company, and as a nucleus about which to gather his men, he selected a squad of twelve. These being thoroughly drilled, and competent to assume the duties of officers, he began to gather recruits. Before the close of the first year he had a company of nearly fifty, who made a handsome appearance in a full-dress uniform of gray, rich in brass buttons and gold lace, and, with the exception of the black helmet, similar to that worn at West Point. A fatigue uniform, consisting of a blue blouse and cap was worn by many, although it was not essential. In the spring of 1886 the company gave an exhibition drill that was heartily commended by a number of army officers who were present. An elaborate programme had been arranged for the Commencement day of 1886, but owing to the inclement weather it was dispensed with. The exercises would have included all the evolutions of the platoon and company, dress, guard mount, and a skirmish drill of twenty rounds. The postponement of this event was most unfortunate, as the cadets would have made an excellent showing, having made wonderful progress under the tuition of Lieutenant Squiers.

There was no perceptible increase in numbers the next year, but the company had acquired a greater familiarity with the movements and evolutions, and the students in general began to look with more favor on the new institution, toward which a feeling of distrust, not unusual in cases of similar innovations, had been engendered among the non-cadets. Through the energetic work of Lieutenant Squiers the company rapidly advanced, and on Commencement-day, 1887, an exhibition drill, similar to that planned for the year previous, was given before a large concourse of people, who heartily applauded the efforts of the embryo soldiers.

The success of the military training was beginning to take effect on those who still remained without the pale, for a glance at the catalogue of the following year shows that their numbers during that time had increased more than twofold. It was even deemed advisable to separate the students of the Preparatory department from the others and form them into a second company, to be drilled by the officers of the first company. The uniform of the second company was altered, the full-dress coat, the helmet, and the long trousers were discarded, and the blouse, fatigue cap, and knee-breeches of gray substituted. A smaller rifle was procured for them, and thenceforth they were entirely separated from the cadets of the Senior division.

The year 1888–89 saw the most complete change the military organization had yet experienced. From a handful of forty-five or fifty, the membership bounded suddenly up to one hundred and fifty. The full-dress coat and helmet were dropped, as they had been the year before at St. John's Hall, and the blouse and fatigue cap, with the gray trousers, constituted the uniform. The corps was divided into four companies, and the spring of 1889 saw an orderly, well-drilled battalion in the field. Lieutenant Squiers, whose interest in the corps had increased, if that were possible, with the increase of interest on the part of the boys, presented a handsome stand of colors to be competed for by the four companies. Lieutenant Price, U. S. A., acted as

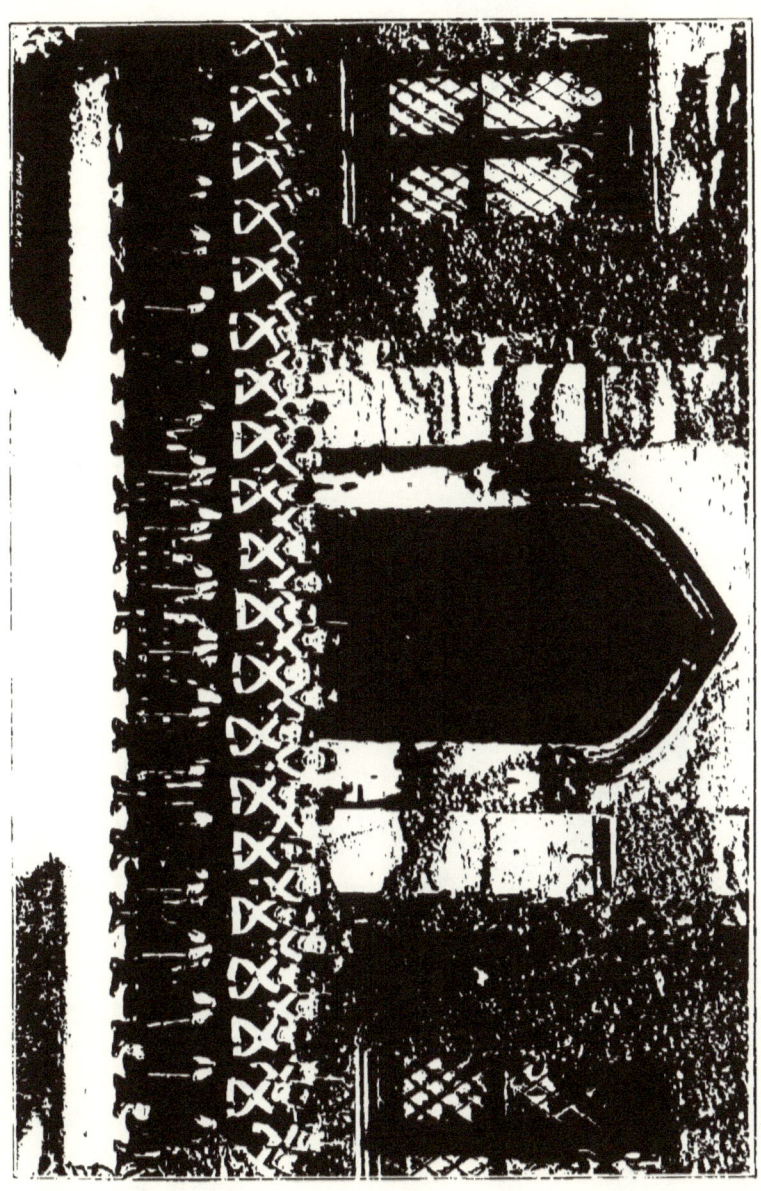

judge on this occasion of the competition drill for these colors, and they were awarded to Company B, Cadet Captain Marrin. The drill this year, as on former occasions, was one of the features of the Commencement-day exercises.

The next year was for the battalion a repetition of the success of 1889. The cadet corps was now firmly established, the antipathy of the students had given way entirely to enthusiasm for the new popular drill, and a spirit of emulation had been engendered by the competition among the companies that was working wonders. The honor of being color company was earned this year by Company D, Cadet Captain Burrow, and the laurels snatched from Company B. The dress parade was held as usual on Commencement-day.

The scholastic year of 1890–91 opened auspiciously for the cadets, and Lieutenant Squiers was once more at his post. He did not remain long at Fordham, however, for as the trouble with the Sioux Indians, which had been brewing for several months, broke out about that time into open warfare, the Lieutenant forwarded a request to the War Department to be assigned to duty with his regiment, which was then at Pine Ridge. The answer came shortly, granting the request, relieving him from duty at Fordham, and directing him to join his regiment in the field. The sorrow at Fordham for his departure was general and loudly expressed, but he felt that when his regiment was in active service in the field of battle, his duty lay there, and like a true soldier he answered the call of duty. His friends were gratified, however, a short time later, when the news arrived that he had been promoted to a first lieutenancy.

Lieutenant Squiers's successor to the post of military

instructor at St. John's appeared in January, 1891, in the person of Second Lieutenant Clarence R. Edwards, First United States Infantry. Lieutenant Edwards is a graduate of West Point, a thorough and efficient officer, and has shown himself, by his management of the military department at Fordham, to be a worthy successor to Lieutenant Squiers. Since his arrival several slight changes have been made in the uniform of the battalion. For dress occasions, a white helmet has been substituted for the fatigue cap, white leggings have been introduced, and other slight alterations effected which all go to improve the general appearance of the corps.

The St. John's Cadets came prominently before the public view on two occasions during the month of May, 1891, on each of which they carried themselves in a way to reflect credit on the institution which they represent. On May 17th, they formed the guard of honor to His Grace Archbishop Corrigan, at the laying of the corner-stone of the new diocesan seminary at Valentine Hill, South Yonkers; and on Decoration-day, the same month, under command of Lieutenant Edwards, they marched, over one hundred and fifty strong, in the parade in New York. They were in excellent form, and won rounds of applause all along the line of march.

The Cadet corps has now become a recognized branch of the course at Fordham. By having a battalion of one hundred and fifty cadets, the detail is secured, while the excellent showing made on exhibition days, and the favorable reports rendered by the Inspector, will serve to strengthen the assurance of a continuation of the privilege. The battalion will take a prominent part in the Jubilee exercises.

Hon. MORGAN J. O'BRIEN.

CHAPTER XIII.

THE COLLEGE SOCIETIES.—THE PARTHENIAN SODALITY.
—THE HISTORICAL AND DEBATING SOCIETIES. — THE
ALUMNI ASSOCIATION.

ONE of the most attractive features of a college of
the present day, and, to the ordinary observer, that
fraught with most interest, is its student life. To the
general public the routine of study, the standing of the
various classes, the relative merits of different systems
of education, have no interest; its attention is centred
on the students. To most people, there is a glamour
over the life of a college student by which they are
instinctively attracted, and, whether they are college
men or not themselves, they always take an interest in
the college student, his societies, and his sports. Therefore, in writing the history of a college we must not
lose sight of so important an item.

Of the Fordham societies, that which, on account of
its age, its character, and the ends it has in view, is certainly the most notable, will occupy our attention first.
We have reference to the Parthenian Sodality. This
sodality is affiliated with the Roman *Prima Primaria,*
under the invocation of the Purification of the Blessed
Virgin Mary and the Patronage of St. Aloysius. It
was established February 2, 1837, at St. Mary's,
Ky., and is therefore four years older than the college itself. When the Jesuit fathers came to Fordham
in 1846, the sodality came with them, and has con-

9

tinued its work without interruption until the present day. The place was changed—nothing more. The minute-book notes the transfer from St. Mary's to Fordham, and goes on with the record of the next meeting as if nothing extraordinary had occurred. Father Legouais, who was director at St. Mary's, continued in the office at Fordham; and several of the students who had been members accompanied the Jesuits to St. John's and continued in the sodality at the latter place.

The sodality was founded by Father Chazelle, the first Jesuit president of St. Mary's, and during its first year he acted as director. At the end of that time he resigned the post to Father Legouais, who continued as director until 1848, two years after their arrival at Fordham. He was succeeded by Father Duranquet, who in 1850 gave way to Father Bernard O'Reilly. After him came Father Smarius, Father Murphy, Father Larkin, Father Gresselin, Father Ronayne, and Father Meagher. Father Ronayne again took charge, and was in turn succeeded by Father Dealy, in 1864. The following year Father Cunningham entered into office, and was followed by Father Fleck, Messrs. Jones, Doherty, Campbell; Fathers Custin, Doucet, Treanor, Flynn, Kenny, Halpin, O'Reilly, Becker, O'-Leary; Messrs. Van Rensselaer and O'Rourke, and again Father Flynn, each holding office only a year, with one or two exceptions.

In September, 1886, the Reverend T. J. A. Freeman took control and held office for two years. At the end of that time it passed into the charge of Mr. George A. Mulry, whose failing health obliged him to resign his charge in the spring of the following year. Before the close of the year he had passed to the reward of his saintly life. His death was a sad blow to the students of Fordham, for he had won countless friends by his gentle, winning ways. Even the most flippant and frivolous were impressed by his holiness, his amiability, and his zeal in the cause of everything that was good. The records of the sodality bear a set of resolutions, in which the sodality expresses its " deep sorrow for the loss of one who, on so many titles, had merited their esteem and love."

Mr. Mulry's term was finished by the Reverend James P. Fagan, and the following year the directorship passed to the Reverend Lawrence Kavanagh, with whom it has remained ever since.

The first name that appears on the list of members of the sodality is that of Michael Driscoll, whose remarkable career we have referred to in another chapter. Further on we meet the names of John Ryan, Walter Hill, Michael Nash, and Fred. Wm. Gockeln, all of whom became in after years distinguished members of the Society of Jesus. Sylvester H. Rosecrans, afterward Bishop of Columbus, William Keegan, James Hughes, now V.-G. of the Hartford Diocese, Michael and Lawrence O'Connor, William Plowden Morrogh, David A. Merrick, Martin T. and James McMahon, James R. O'Beirne, Thomas B. Connery, John R. Hassard, Richard Brennan, and Joseph J. Marrin, are among the well-known names to be found on the rolls of the sodality. Father Driscoll was the first prefect, and among his successors were Fathers Ryan, Hill, Gockeln, and Morrogh, Judge Dodge, Dr. Brennan, John R. Hassard, P. A. Hargous, Francis V. Oliver, Dean Mooney, Ignatius McManus, Father

Keveney, S.J., Judge O'Brien, Father Quin, S.J., and the late lamented Father William A. Dunphy.

February 2, 1887, the fiftieth anniversary of the founding of the sodality was commemorated by the erection of a bronze statue, of the Blessed Virgin in the quadrangle before the entrance to the chapel. The exercises opened with mass at 6.30 A.M., celebrated by Father Freeman, director of the Sodality, at which all received Holy Communion. The unveiling and blessing of the statue, which was to take place at 9 A.M., followed by solemn mass, was postponed until May 1st, on account of the inclemency of the weather. A literary circle was held in the afternoon, and a sermon, followed by solemn benediction, concluded the exercises. The statue was solemnly blessed on May 1st by the Very Reverend R. W. Brady, provincial of the New York-Maryland Province.

On October 2, 1847, the second sodality was formed, under the name of the Sodality of the Holy Angels, but merely as a branch of the Parthenian Sodality, the treasury and library being common. In 1852 it was entirely separated from the parent organization, and has remained so ever since. In 1856 or 1857, the Third Division Sodality was formed under the patronage of St. Stanislaus, but it seems to have been more widely separated from the others, because the sodalist from Third Division was obliged to renew his act of consecration on entering the other body. The sodality for externs was established in 1889, and regularly aggregated to the *Primaria* at Rome. Mr. Francis J. Lamb, S.J., was its first director.

Next in point of years to the sodalities comes the Debating Society. Debating societies are among the

Walks and Fountain in the Rear of St. John's Hall, Fordham.

oldest of organized societies, and seem to have always been considered necessary adjuncts to institutions of learning. There is not, perhaps, a college or high school in the country that has not an organization wherein questions of moment are discussed and sifted.

Fordham was without a society of this kind until 1854. There was, it is true, a tradition of a society called the " Crestomathian," which was said to have existed in Fordham in days gone by, but no one in the college at the time had any recollection of it. In one of the upper rooms of the " castle " was an old closet, securely locked, and which no one had ever seen open. Across the door of this mysterious closet was the cabalistic word "Crestomathian." This was supposed to contain the treasures of the pre-historic association, and when the St. John's Debating Society was organized, in 1854, the latter deeming itself entitled to the property of all similar defunct societies in the house, decided to seize on the treasure supposed to have been hoarded for so many years in the dingy little closet. But the search revealed nothing. The closet was empty.

The St. John's Debating Society was organized, as we have stated, in the fall of 1854. According to the constitution, the president was a member of the faculty appointed by that body. The vice-president was elected for the whole year, the other officers semi-annually. The Reverend C. M. Smarius, S.J., was the first president, General McMahon, vice-president, and John R. Hassard, recording secretary. The membership was limited to the classes of Philosophy and Rhetoric. A gold badge was adopted by the society, in the form of a shield, and in the centre, which was open, was pendent a maltese cross with the Greek letters Π Φ K N

inscribed thereon.   On the reverse was the name of the
wearer and the date of his class.   The initials stood for
the motto Πολεμέω φίλως καὶ νικάω.

The meetings were held weekly, on Sunday evening,
in the reading-room which was then in the basement of
the "castle." Two public debates were given every
year, one by the Philosophy class and the other by the
members of the class of Rhetoric.   These public events
were held regularly until about 1878, when they were
reduced to one every year, and a short time after they
were dropped altogether.   In 1884 they were restored,
but in the fall of 1886 the Debating Society was
changed into the House of Commons, and the public
debates were discontinued.   By this change, which was
effected by desire of Father Campbell, the society was
resolved into the form of a legislative body in every respect similar to the British House of Parliament.   This
change was made to encourage extempore speaking, and
give the student the habit of "thinking on his feet."
Its success was phenomenal.   The members fell readily
into the new methods of procedure, and the advantages
over the old form were soon made apparent.   It is to
be regretted, however, that in making the change some
provision was not made for the perpetuation of the
badge which had been worn by so many generations of
students.   It was dropped that year, and has never been
restored.

In the fall of 1888 another change was made, from
the St. John's House of Commons to the St. John's
Senate.   The same form of debate was preserved, however, and the change was only in the name, the officers,
and a few minor details.   It was made through motives of patriotism.   This state of affairs did not last

long, for two years later we find the Senate abolished altogether, and the old St. John's Debating Society once more restored.

The Historical Association was formed in 1862, the first meeting being held on March 16th, on which occasion the president of the college, Father Thébaud, addressed the members on the object and aim of the society. This organization differed from the Debating Society, inasmuch as all the members of the Classes of Philosophy and Rhetoric, to which it was limited, were not obliged to enter. On the contrary, the candidate for admission must prove his title to membership by presenting an essay which was passed upon by a committee appointed for that purpose. His admission or rejection depended on the report of that committee. This rule remained in force until the year 1887–88, when, for some unaccountable reason, the association was suspended. It was reorganized the following year through Father Scully, and the constitution amended so as to admit the classes of Philosophy, Rhetoric, and Special Science, *in toto*.

The first director of this association, or, as he is styled, the Honorary President, was Father Doucet. The other officers for the first year were : A. T. Lynch, president; William Collins, vice-president; John Gafney, corresponding secretary; R. L. Spalding, recording secretary; James Olwell, treasurer, and William Doherty, librarian.

A public lecture is given every year under the auspices of the association by some distinguished scholar, writer, or orator. A gold medal, valued at $50, for the best biographical essay, which originated with Archbishop Hughes, and which is donated every year by some friend of the college, is competed for by the members who are of the graduating class.

The Alumni Association of St. John's College is among the oldest of the societies connected with that institution, but as no record of its meetings or transactions has ever been kept, it is impossible to fix the exact date of its organization. Memory is proverbially treacherous, and it is never safe to base statements of historical facts on memory only, especially when it extends over a period of thirty or forty years; but, as in this case we have only the memory of some of the older members to guide us, we must make the most of it. As closely as can be calculated, the association was founded about 1860. It did little more than hold its annual meeting on Commencement-day, and elect officers for the ensuing year, until about 1882 it awoke to greater activity, and established a fund to provide a purse of $50 annually, as a prize for the best essay in English literature in the classes of Philosophy, Rhetoric, and Belles-lettres.

In the spring of 1888 the Alumni Association again came forward in the movement for the erection of the Hughes monument. The matter came up in the course of a conversation between Reverend Fathers Scully, Loyzance, and E. F. Slattery, '72, and the credit of the suggestion is due to the Reverend Joseph Loyzance, S.J., and Reverend E. F. Slattery, '72, of New York. At a meeting of the committee held shortly afterward, Father Slattery offered a resolution that the Alumni Association undertake the task of collecting $10,000 for the erection of a bronze statue to the dead archbishop. The resolution was adopted and circulars issued notifying the members of the action of the committee.

The work of preparing the model was entrusted to Mr. William Rudolf O'Donovan, an able and enthusiastic sculptor, and the casting of the bronze figure was given to Mr. Maurice J. Power, of New York.

The plan of erecting the statue in 1889, as was at first intended, was soon abandoned, as it was impossible to collect a sufficient amount in so short a time, and it was decided to postpone the ceremony until the jubilee celebration in 1891. At this point Judge Morgan J. O'Brien, '72, now president of the Alumni Association, and the Reverend James J. Flood, '68, of New York, interested themselves in the movement, and it was mainly through their efforts that a sufficient sum of money was raised to warrant the beginning of the work. Judge O'Brien has been indefatigable in this cause, and his efforts have been crowned with success. The statue will be ready for the ceremony of unveiling by June 24th.

CHAPTER XIV.

Not by any means the least important of the students' societies of Fordham College is the Dramatic Association. The college is in reality the natural home of the drama. It is to the early universities and monasteries that we owe the preservation of the drama. In these institutions it was preserved in its purest form, and the miracle plays of the middle ages, which were performed at the colleges and monasteries throughout Europe, were witnessed in a spirit which amounted al most to religious fervor. We know that in the early days of the English drama it was a feature of college life, for *Hamlet* says to *Polonius :*

"My lord, you played once i' the university, you say."
Polonius. "That did I, my lord ; and was accounted a good actor."

Moreover, the *Ratio Studiorum* of the Jesuits, which is centuries old, recommends the practice of giving plays in the colleges under the Jesuit rule.

The custom of giving plays at Fordham extends back, as indeed many of the customs do, to the earlier days of St. Mary's College. Father Chazelle, the first Jesuit president of St. Mary's, and one of the first Jesuits of that colony to arrive in this country, introduced dra-

matic entertainments at that place. The first play put
upon the boards was an original drama from the pen
of Father Chazelle himself, entitled "Red Hawk." It
was produced before a numerous audience and caused
a genuine sensation. The theatre chosen for this performance indeed indicated a return to the primitive traditions of the drama. "At that time," writes the Reverend Walter H. Hill, S.J., "the college was partly
surrounded by thickly wooded primeval groves, a suitable spot in the forest was chosen for the stage, which
could be seen by the spectators from a rising slope at
the front, and a whole acre was covered with seats for
the audience. The large stage was adorned with drap-
ery of high colors; there were suitable changes of scenery also. So well adapted to the purpose was Father
Chazelle's ideal, that it was strictly adhered to ever
afterward, until our fathers left St. Mary's, in 1846;
during all which period the annual exhibitions, with
the accompanying drama, took place at a well-chosen
spot in the wild woods."

The second play performed on this woodland stage
was entitled "Benedict Arnold, the Traitor," the chief
sensation of which, Father Hill tells us, was the hang-
ing of Major André on the stage, "so that all could see
the ignominious end of a British spy."

After the removal to Fordham, however, dramatics
appear to have been neglected for many years. Until
1855 the idea of a dramatic performance was treated
with ridicule by the older students and relegated to the
small boys, as being better suited to their youth and
immaturity. A few of the younger boys banded together and attempted to arrange entertainments. But
they always chose the most ambitious themes for their

performances, and their efforts were so crude and puerile as to be hardly worthy of attention. In the fall of 1855, however, a change took place. Father Tellier, who was then president, encouraged the classes of Belles-lettres and Classics to unite in giving dramatic entertainments.

At this time Mr. Charles M. Walcott, who is now a prominent member of the Lyceum Theatre Company, of New York, was a student in the latter class, and he was made Stage Manager. Mr. Walcott came of a theatrical family, and was therefore, " to the manner born." He signalized his elevation to that important post by obtaining a drop curtain from New York, painted specially for St. John's and representing a scene on the Hudson. This and the scenery, which the boys constructed themselves, were adjusted to the platform at the north end of the study-hall for every performance, and at the conclusion stored away until another play called them forth again from their retreat. The first play given under his management, and the first too for which a printed programme was used, was given on December 3, 1855. On this occasion " Henry IV " and " The Seven Clerks," were presented, with Mr. Walcott as *Falstaff* in the one, and *Mynheer Hans Hoogdfit* in the other. Between the pieces, so the programme says, Mr. C. Walcott sang a " Comic Song." The following July a second " Dramatic Exhibition " was given, the programme of which informs us that the St. John's Dramatic Society " have spared no pains to select for the occasion plays calculated to entertain the curious and the learned." The audiences in those days were evidently partial to long programmes, for this one contains Byron's tragedy " Werner," a farce, "To Paris and Back for £5," and "The Inn of Abbeville."

"Richard II.," "Macbeth," and "Julius Cæsar" followed in quick succession, and then there is a blank in the record until 1867, when we find that a comedy was substituted for the musical entertainment given on St. Patrick's Day by the Cæcilia Society. Gradually the dramatic entertainments superseded the public debates, until 1871, when the present Dramatic Association was organized. The stage was built in the First Division study-hall, and the curtain and proscenium painted by an Italian scholastic who was stopping at the college. After 1872 the regular number of plays was given as at the present day, Thanksgiving Day, Christmas, Washington's Birthday, and St. Patrick's Day. Shrovetide and the Rector's Day were fixed on as occasions for dramatic entertainments in after years, the latter during Father Shea's presidency.

Since the organization of the Dramatic Association a complete record has been kept of the society's doings, so we have no difficulty in tracing its very successful career since that time. During its nineteen years of life and activity it has produced a large number of plays, of infinite variety as to class and character. The most notable successes of recent years have been "The Man in the Iron Mask," in '80; "Damon and Pythias," in '81; "King John," in '82; "Henry IV.," Part I., in '83; "Henry IV.," Part II., in '84; "Merchant of Venice," in '85; and "Hamlet," in '87. The present president of the college, Father Scully, was for many years moderator of the Dramatic Association, as were also Father Halpin, Father Finnegan, Father Fargis, and Father Cassidy, now president of St. Peter's College,

Jersey City.   Mr. John F. Quirk, S.J., Mr. L. Eugene French, S.J., Mr. Joseph H. Smith, S.J., and Mr. George A. Pettit, S.J., who now rule the destinies of the association, are among those of later years.

Many old members of the Dramatic Association are now playing important rôles in the more serious drama of life.   Edward C. O'Brien, who made such a success of "The Man in the Iron Mask," is now a well-known lawyer in New York, and is secretary of the Alumni Association.   His brother, M. H. O'Brien, and Peter A. Hendrick, have also found success in the practice of the law.   William McTammany, since deceased, and Lawrence McNamara, of New York, turned their attention to the healing art, and C. M. Walcott, the pioneer among Fordham actors, Fred Williams, George Hill, and Stephen Murphy, of later years, now tread the boards in real earnest, and are, or promise soon to be, well-known figures on the professional stage.   Many are found in the ranks of the clergy, as the Reverend T. F. McLaughlin, C. J. Clifford, S.J., the Reverend William J. McGurk; and then there was Austin O'Malley, Andrew G. Heyl, Frank Casey, since deceased, Dr. T. J. Dunn, Dr. J. N. Butler, and a host of others.

Each in his turn has made his last exit from Fordham; some have passed forever from the scenes of this life, but the memory of all is still fresh in the scenes of their triumphs, and their names and their deeds will be handed down from generation to generation.

The history of journalism at Fordham, previous to the establishment of *The Fordham Monthly*, presents a series of vicissitudes.   The first effort of which we have any record was the *Goose-Quill*, which made its first appearance in 1853, during the presidency of Father Larkin. The paper was edited by "Ham," but who Ham was remained a profound secret for many years. It is now a well-known fact that the editors of the *Goose-Quill* were John R. G. Hassard, Arthur Francis, and Martin T. McMahon, of the class of '55. The *Goose-Quill* was a monthly publication of twenty-eight or thirty pages of foolscap carefully written, for in those days they could not get it printed. The pages were headed and ruled like a printed paper; Father Gareschć engrossed the heading, and Mr. Hassard, who was a neat, careful penman, copied out the reading matter.

Father Larkin, who had very conservative ideas on such subjects, was opposed to the enterprise from the first, and merely tolerated it. He would not allow the editors to have it printed or circulated outside of the college, and for a long time withheld permission to post it in the reading-room. The proceedings in the sanctum of the *Goose-Quill* were carried on with the utmost secrecy. Besides the editors themselves and some of the fathers, no one knew who Ham was. In the extension which connected the study-hall wing, now the chapel wing, with the " castle," was a room which in later years served as a sacristy. Father Gockeln, who was vice-president at the time, furnished the editors with a key by which they could open the door leading from the study-hall into this room. Here, in perfect security, the *Goose-Quill* was prepared. A box was placed in the reading-room in which contributions addressed to Ham could be placed, and as Hassard and McMahon were officers and carried keys to the reading-room, they could procure the letters without fear of discovery. In 1855, on the graduation of Messrs. Hassard, Francis, and McMahon, the paper was turned over by them to P. A. Hargous, Henry Smith, and Thomas A. O'Connor, but in a very short time ceased to appear.

One or two desultory efforts were made within the next few years to establish a successor to the *Goose-Quill*, but they all failed. *Sem, The Collegian,* and a paper called *The Spy,* published on Second Division by Mr. J. J. Costello, '62, of Cayuga, N. Y., were the results of some of these efforts. The last-named journal died after the second issue. Since that time there is no sign of a journal until the appearance of the first number of *The Fordham College Monthly,* in November, 1882. The public, in this case represented by the Fordham students, always chary about taking up and encouraging any new undertaking, made no exception to its usual mode of procedure in the case of *The Fordham College Monthly.* As a consequence the first board of editors had a hard struggle to place the journal on a solid footing and win the support of the other students.* That they succeeded is evident from the present handsome appearance of *The Fordham Monthly.†*

And before we conclude, a word about athletics at Fordham. St. John's has won renown in the athletic world only in one field, viz., base-ball. In every other branch, except perhaps foot-ball, in which she is fast

---

* The first board of editors consisted of Francis D. Dowley, '83, editor-in-chief; James N. Butler, '84, assistant; John R. Murphy, business manager; and as associate editors, Charles Hoban, '85, Joseph W. Thoron, '83, William P. O'Malley, '84, and Bernard F. McManus, '85.

† The name was changed from *The Fordham College Monthly* to *The Fordham Monthly* in December, 1885.

BALL-FIELD AND CAMPUS, ST. JOHN'S COLLEGE, FORDHAM, SHOWING TOBOGGAN SLIDE.

coming to the front, Fordham has yet to win her spurs. An organized athletic association has only existed within the last few years, and then its success has been rather doubtful. But there is yet hope. With the shining example of the Base-Ball Association and the still flickering light of foot-ball success to guide it and lend it hope, a well-organized athletic association has everything to encourage it. The base-ball team, for so many years known as the Rose Hill team, but of late known by the more significant title of Fordham, won its way to fame many years ago, and by its recent glorious victories has proven its ability to hold against all-comers the proud position it has attained. What has been achieved in the base-ball field can be achieved elsewhere, and we feel confident that the day of its attainment is not far distant.

We have here reviewed, briefly it may be, the events that go to make up the history of the first half-century of Fordham College. We found it a solitary farm-house situated in a wide unsettled tract of land; we take leave of it a group of magnificent buildings in the centre of a growing community. We found it a struggling Catholic school in " an unfinished house in a field; " we take leave of a flourishing university increasing its classes, elevating its standard, and extending its facilities year by year.

What better evidence could we desire of the energy and devotion of that little community that, guided by the hand of God, came from the wilds of a half-settled country to take charge of and direct what was destined one day to become the foremost Catholic college in the

10

country? What more eloquent tribute could be offered
to the wisdom and foresight of its venerable founder,
in entrusting its care to such able hands, than the success with which the enterprise has met? They need
no monument; they need no graven tablet to perpet-
uate the memory of their work to future generations.
This, the fruit of their labor, is their monument, founded on a solid rock, *ære perennius.*

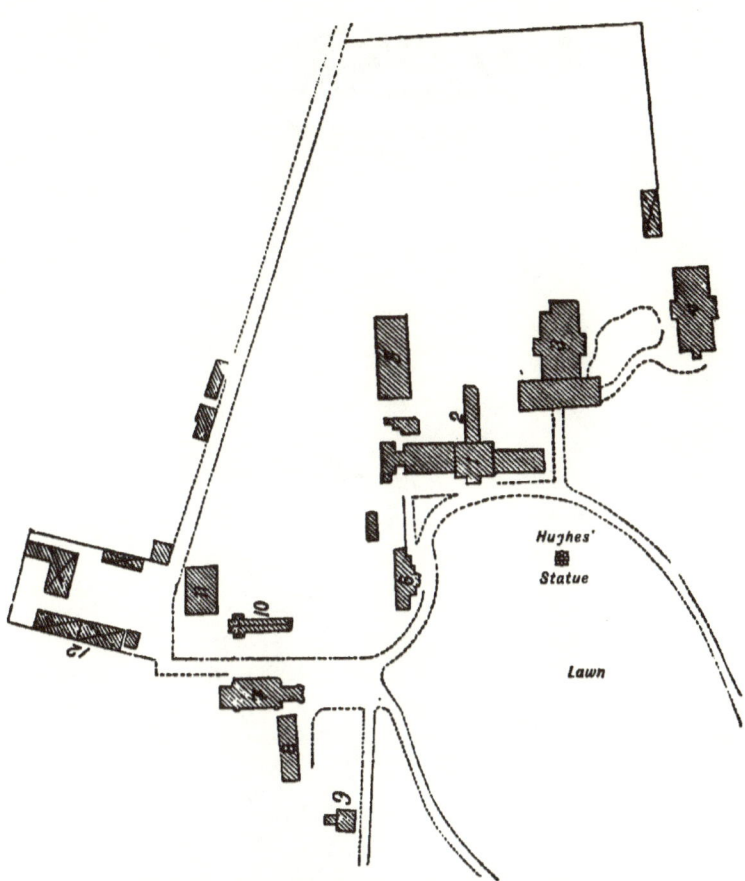

(1) Old Manor containing President's and Treasurer's Office, Parlor Students'
    and Faculty Dining Rooms, Students' Chapel, Professors Rooms.

(2) Library and Wardrobe.

(3) Faculty Building and Seniors' Hall.

(4) Science Hall, Museum, Laboratories, Engine Room.

(5) Juniors' Hall.

(6) Old Manor House, now used as Infirmary.

(7) College Church.

(8) St. John's Hall (Preparatory).

(9) Rodrigue Cottage.

(10) Conservatory and Hot-house.

(11) College Cemetery.

(12) Barns.

APPENDIX.

BELOW is appended a list of the principal donations received by the college, with the names of the donors :

May 18, 1866, a Friend of the college...............	$400 00
September, 1867, Catharine Collery.................	200 00
A second donation	100 00
April, 1874, Mary McDonough D'Arcy	503 00
January, 1876, Sir Edward Kenny..................	563 75
January, 1878, Sir Edward Kenny..................	500 00
September, 1884, a Friend to the Rev. P. T. Dealy, for the college walk..............................	1,000 00
July, 1885, a Friend to Father Dealy, for frescoing the students' refectory............................	600 00
August, 1888, the Estate of the Rev. F. H. McGovern, S.J., for fitting up St. John's Hall..............	5,102 25
November, 1889, Bernard J. McGrann, A.M., Lancaster, Pa., to the Rev. John Scully, S.J...............	2,000 00
December, 1889, John McKeown, Washington, Pa....	1,000 00
November, 1890, John Whalen, A.M................	1,000 00
December, 1890, a Friend to Father Scully	500 00
1891, a Friend, for new building	15,000 00
June, 1891, Ann Cassidy, for altars................	2,500 00
May, 1891, Patrick Golden, Parsons, Pa., through James J. Walsh, A.M., S.J., for St. Joseph's window in the new chapel.................................	300 00
June, 1891, Estate of the late Patrick Carney, of Mott Haven, to educate one student for the priesthood.	5,000 00
1889–91, Estate of the late Bryan McCahill, through Thomas J. McCahill, A.M., to educate a student for the priesthood	340 00
1890–91, Lieutenant Herbert G. Squiers, U.S.A., to educate two boys..............................	660 00

LIST OF CONTRIBUTORS TO THE HUGHES STATUE.

Eugene Kelly	$1,000 00
Hon. Wm. R. Grace	250 00
Hon. W. C. Whitney	250 00
Henry McAleenan	250 00
Peter Doelger	250 00
Hon. Edward Cooper	250 00
O. B. Potter	250 00
Thos. F. Ryan	250 00
Bishop John Loughlin	200 00
D. C. Connell	200 00
Hon. Theo. W. Meyers	150 00
Hon. Hugh J. Grant	150 00
John F. Haben, McKeesport, Pa	101 50
Archbishop Corrigan	100 00
Rev. John J. Hughes	200 00
Rev. J. J. Flood	100 00
Hon. M. J. O'Brien	100 00
Robert McCafferty	100 00
Thos. Macmannus, Chihuahua, Mex	100 00
Wm. H. Hurst	100 00
Hon. Gunning S. Bedford	100 00
C. C. Baldwin	100 00
Jos. P. Payten	100 00
David McClure	100 00
Frederick R. Coudert	100 00
John O'Neill	100 00
Hon. Henry D. Purroy	100 00
George Ehret	100 00
Francis O'Neill	100 00
Daniel Lavery, 594 Ninth Av	100 00
Hon. Jos. J. O'Donohue, 5 East Sixty-ninth St	100 00
M. P. Breslin, 114 East Seventieth St	100 00
Thos. Kelly	100 00
Henry Amy	100 00
James J. Doherty, West Forty-sixth St	225 00
T. R. Crawford	100 00

Hon. Richard O'Gorman	$100 00
Major John Byrne................................	100 00
Rev. D. A. Merrick, Rector St. Francis Xavier's........	100 00
Thos. H. O'Connor	100 00
Thomas J. McCahill	100 00
Jacob Ruppert....................................	100 00
Rev. Patrick McGovern, Croton.....................	100 00
John O'Donohue	50 00
Maurice Ahearn..................................	50 00
F. C. O'Reilly, New Jersey.........................	50 00
Rev. William McNulty	50 00
St. John's College (Alumni Prize)...................	50 00
H. K. Doherty	50 00
Mr. Walsh, Parsons, Pa., for his son, Jas. J. Walsh, S.J...	50 00
Rev. Wm. Keagan, V.-G............................	50 00
Rev. J. J. Doherty (additional)	80 00
Rev. John Gleason................................	50 00
L. J. Callanan	50 00
Peter McGinnis..................................	50 00
John Reilly, East Fourteenth St.....................	50 00
Thos. Dunn, Fordham	50 00
Hon. James Fitzgerald.............................	50 00
Hon. John D. Crimmins............................	50 00
Edward Stokes...................................	50 00
Michael Fitzsimmons	50 00
Rev. John F. Kearney.............................	50 00
John B. Manning.................................	75 00
Patrick Farrelly.................................	50 00
Leo Schlesinger..................................	50 00
Excelsior Council, C.B.L., P. J. Kennedy, Park & Tilford, Fifty-ninth St. and Fifth Av..............	50 00
Hon. Chauncey M. Depew...........................	50 00
Edw. C. Sheehy, Eleventh St. and Third Av...........	50 00
Henry Clausen, Forty-seventh St. and Second Av.......	50 00
Edmond J. Curry, 1510 Third Av....................	50 00
Major Edward Duffy	50 00
Patrick Kiernan..................................	50 00
John Mack	50 00
Cornelius Callahan	50 00

Rev. Sylvester Malone $50 00
John A. Sullivan 50 00
James McMahon, Brooklyn, N. Y..................... 50 00
Edward Schell 50 00
John Woods, Jersey City, N. J...................... 40 00
James Meehan...................................... 25 00
Eugene Durnin 25 00
P. A. Hendrick 25 00
J. Mulleen 25 00
Rev. James Fitzjames 25 00
Hon. T. R. Sheil, William's Bridge 25 00
Rev. Father Fitzharris 25 00
John J. Brady 25 00
Rev. John Weir 25 00
Rev. M. A. Hallahan, Ticonderoga, N. Y.............. 25 00
Very Rev. Jas. S. Lynch, V.-G., Syracuse, N. Y......... 25 00
Rev. John A. McKenna 25 00
Rev. M. J. McEvoy 25 00
Hon. Honore Mercier 25 00
Rev. J. F. Flood, Chicago 25 00
Rev. Jas. J. Flood 25 00
Dr. T. J. Dunn..................................... 25 00
Rev. John Quinn, Collinsville, Conn................... 25 00
Rev. Paul T. Carew, Newark 25 00
Patrick Walsh 25 00
John Slattery, Fifty-third St........................ 25 00
Rev. D. O'Conor, Dobb's Ferry 25 00
Rev. M. J. Lavelle.................................. 25 00
A. L. Ashman, Sinclair House 25 00
L. J. Callanan, Jr. 25 00
James J. Callanan 25 00
James A. O'Gorman 25 00
Rev. Dr. Wood 25 00
Edward C. O'Brien 25 00
Hon. L. A. Giegerich 25 00
Herman Ridder..................................... 25 00
Henry Hughes, 234 East Thirty-fourth St.............. 25 00
Hon. J. S. Coleman................................. 25 00
Rev. Patrick Kelly.................................. 25 00

Rev. Jos. P. Eagan.....................................	$25 00
Louis F. Haffen	50 00
Louis M. Benziger....................................	25 00
Dr. Wm. J. O'Byrne	25 00
Bro. Anthony, Manhattan College	25 00
F. V. S. Oliver	25 00
Chas. E. Miller	25 00
Wm. Lummis..	25 00
James D. Lynch.......................................	25 00
Hon. James J. Martin.................................	25 00
William H. Seward	25 00
James Olwell	25 00
Patrick Carroll.......................................	25 00
John Murtha	25 00
Very Rev. John M. Farley	25 00
F. P. Carroll...	25 00
Hon. Henry R. Beekman, 111 Broadway.................	25 00
Jos. J. Gleason, 216 East Fiftieth St...................	25 00
Dr. L. J. McNamara, 126 Washington Pl...............	25 00
Jas. Olwell & Co......................................	25 00
John Earley	25 00
John Dnun	25 00
John P. Dunn	25 00
Dominick O'Reilly....................................	25 00
Thos. F. Carr..	25 00
Peter A. Lalor.......................................	25 00
Jas. M. Quigley, 44 Wall St...........................	25 00
Judge Jos. F. Daly	25 00
Fr. Pustet & Co.......................................	25 00
James J. Phelan......................................	25 00
Walter G. Hennessey	25 00
Jos. Dillon	25 00
Dennis A. Spellissey	25 00
J. Fitzpatrick & Co...................................	25 00
B. Muldone..	25 00
Hon. W. L. Brown, Senator...........................	25 00
James Read & Co	25 00
Rev. Nicholas J. Hughes	25 00
Lyceum of St. John's (Evangelist).....................	25 00

Michael J. N. McCaffery	$25 00
Alpin J. Cameron	25 00
Thos. F. Eagan	25 00
John McCann	25 00
Hon. J. Fitzsimmons	25 00
Rev. P. W. Tandy	25 00
Randolph Guggenheimer	25 00
James G. Johnson	25 00
Hon. Thos. F. Gilroy	25 00
Mills & Coleman	25 00
Rev. F. P. Rafferty	20 00
Otto Horwitz, Stewart Building	20 00
Rev. C. B. O'Reilly	20 00
Jos. Leavey	20 00
Mrs. Ann Dyer, Fordham	20 00
Smythe & Ryan	20 00
Dr. W. A. McCreary	20 00
James J. Traynor	20 00
Mrs. J. Combes	20 00
Martin J. Flemming, M.D	20 00
Augustin Daly	20 00
Francis Higgins (additional)	25 00
General M. F. McMahon	15 00
Wm. Farrell	10 00
James J. Larkin	10 00
Mrs. M. L. Flynn	10 00
Nicholas Murphy	10 00
Rev. Wm. A. Dunphy	10 00
" James E. Bobier	10 00
" M. J. McAvoy	25 00
" Thos. Lynch	10 00
T. F. Neville	10 00
Geo. Edebohls, M.D	10 00
Very Rev. James Hughes, V.-G	10 00
C. V. Fornes	10 00
Rev. F. A. Smith, S.J	10 00
S. A. Wall	10 00
Rev. Wm. L. Penny	10 00
M. Donohoe	10 00

Jos. Thoron	$10 00
Dalton Bros	10 00
Felix P. Kremp	10 00
Bryan Laurence	10 00
Geo. M. Curtis, 269 Broadway	10 00
M. Hallinan, 196 West Fourth St	10 00
Mrs. R. W. Montgomery	10 00
A. H. Dundon	10 00
Rev. P. F. McSweeney, D.D	10 00
O. P. Buel	10 00
Rev. H. A. Brann, D.D	10 00
Rev. M. A. Taylor	10 00
G. Herbermann	10 00
P. Donohue	10 00
John J. Rogers	10 00
B. L. Keenally	10 00
Rev. James Nilan	10 00
Rev. Thos. J. McMillan, C.S.P	10 00
William F. Carey	10 00
John H. Hyland	10 00
Rev. I. Meister	10 00
Bernholtz & Son	10 00
Rev. John J. Boyle, West 125th St	10 00
Stoltzenberg & Co	10 00
Mr. P. Brennan	10 00
G. W. Eggleston	5 00
Jas. McDonnell	5 00
Jas. M. Quigley	5 00
C. H. McCusker	5 00
Cash, Oct. 13th (Father Scully)	5 00
Mr. Baley (Mexico)	5 00
Mr. Murtaugh	5 00
P. I. Kelly	5 00
Mrs. Fisher, Bedford Park	5 00
Mrs. Mary Burke, Fordham	5 00
Pope & Klay	5 00
Mr. Biggane	5 00
Anonymous	5 00
John S. O'Meara	5 00

Reynolds Bros.................................... $5 00
Jas. S. Baron 5 00
Talbot & Farjon.................................... 5 00
A. L Beemis 2 00
J. V. Healy.. 1 00
The Daughter of a King........................... 0 10